W9-ASU-625

LUKE

ON THE LOOSE

A TOON BOOK BY

HARRY BLISS

For Delia M.

A JUNIOR LIBRARY GUILD SELECTION
SCHOOL LIBRARY JOURNAL BEST COMICS FOR KIDS 2009
Association for Library Service to Children
GRAPHIC NOVELS READING LIST 2013, 2014, and 2016

Editorial Director: FRANÇOISE MOULY

Book Design: FRANÇOISE MOULY & JONATHAN BENNETT

Colors: FRANÇOISE MOULY & ZEYNEP MEMECAN

A TOON Book™ © 2009 RAW Junior, LLC, 27 Greene Street, New York, NY 10013. TOON Books®, TOON Graphics™,
LITTLE LIT® and TOON Into Reading™ are trademarks of RAW Junior, LLC. All rights reserved. No part of this book may be
used or reproduced in any manner whatsoever without written permission except in the case of brief quotations embodied
in critical articles and reviews. All our books are Smyth Sewn (the highest library-quality binding available) and printed with
soy-based inks on acid-free, woodfree paper harvested from responsible sources. Printed in China by C&C Offset Printing
Co., Ltd. Distributed to the trade by Consortium Book Sales & Distribution, a division of Ingram Content Group; orders (866)
400-5351; ips@ingramcontent.com; www.cbsd.com.

Library of Congress Cataloging-in-Publication Data: Bliss, Harry, 1964-   Luke on the loose : a TOON Book / by
Harry Bliss.p. cm.   Summary: A young boy's fascination with pigeons soon erupts into a full-blown chase around
Central Park, across the Brooklyn Bridge, through a fancy restaurant, and into the sky.   1. Graphic novels [1.
Graphic novels. 2. Pigeons--Fiction. 3. Lost children--Fiction. 4. New York (N.Y.)--Fiction. 5. Humorous stories.] I.
Title.   PZ7.7.B57Lu 2009   741.5'973--dc22   2008035699
             ISBN: 978-1-935179-00-9 (hardcover)   ISBN: 978-1-935179-36-8 (paperback)

19 20 21 22 23 24 C&C 10 9 8 7 6 5 4

www.TOON-BOOKS.com

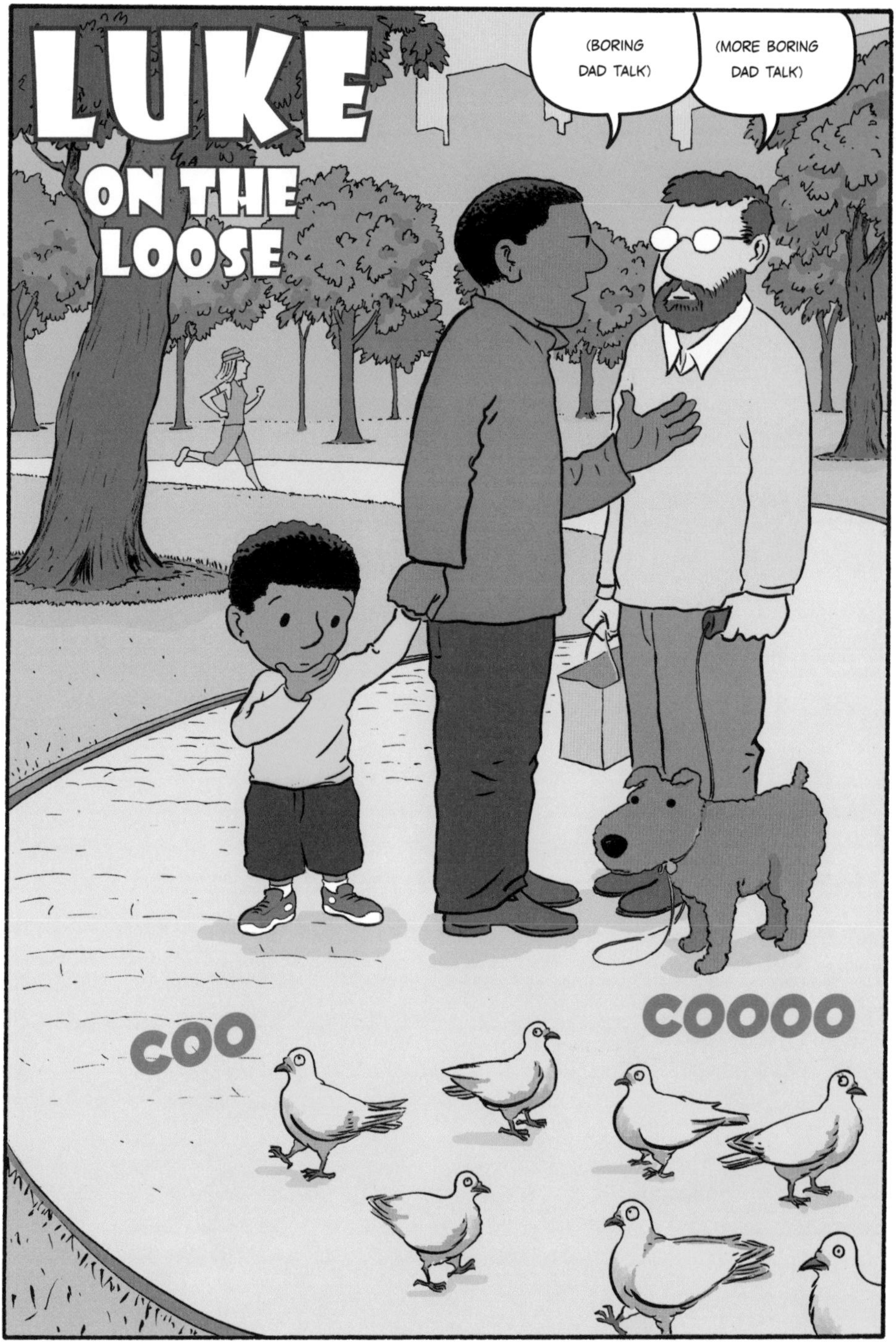
LUKE
ON THE
LOOSE
(BORING DAD TALK)
(MORE BORING DAD TALK)
COO
COOOO

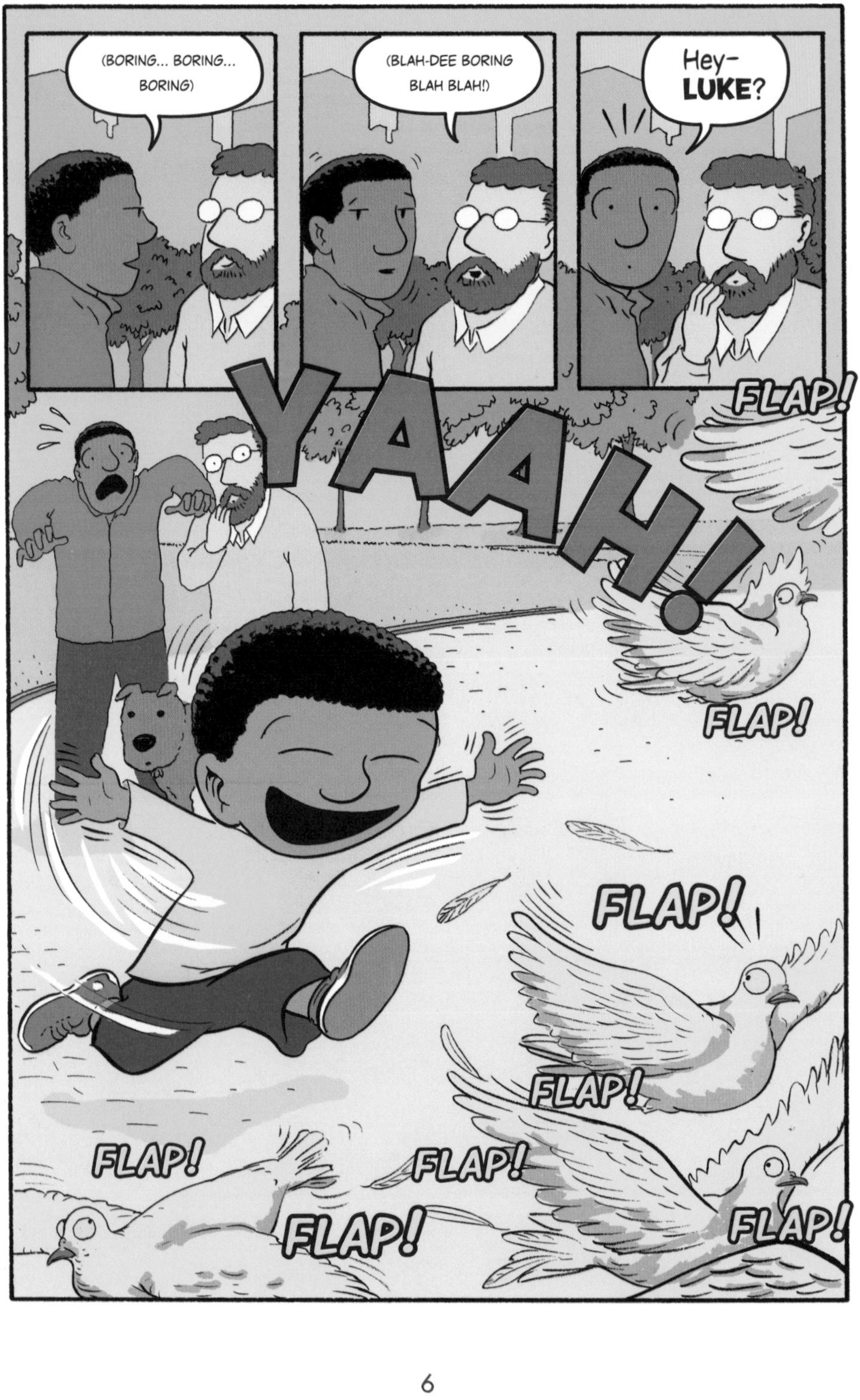
(BORING... BORING... BORING)
(BLAH-DEE BORING BLAH BLAH!)
Hey- LUKE?
YAAAH!
FLAP!
FLAP!
FLAP!
FLAP!
FLAP!
FLAP!
FLAP!
FLAP!

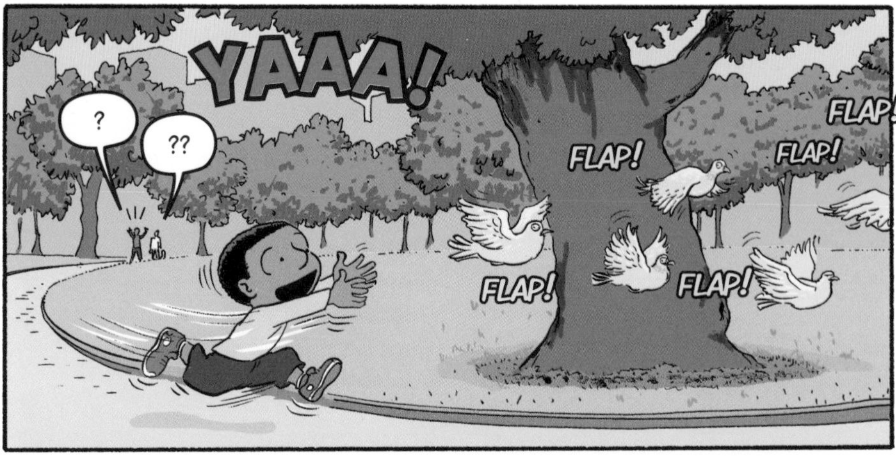
YAAA!
?
??
FLAP!
FLAP!
FLAP!
FLAP!
FLAP!
FLAP!

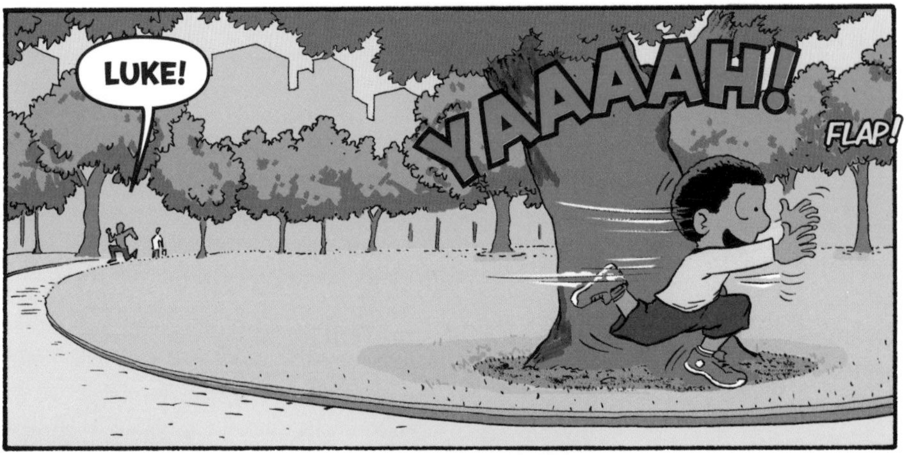
LUKE!
YAAAAAH!
FLAP!

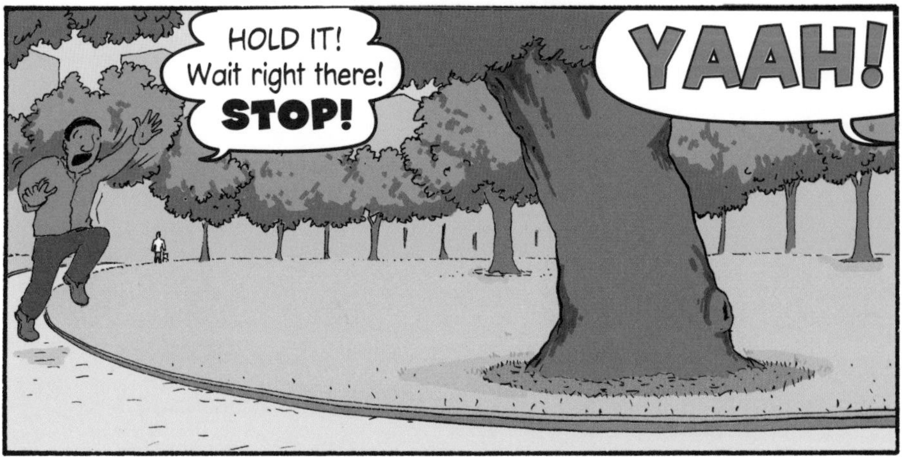
HOLD IT!
Wait right there!
STOP!
YAAH!

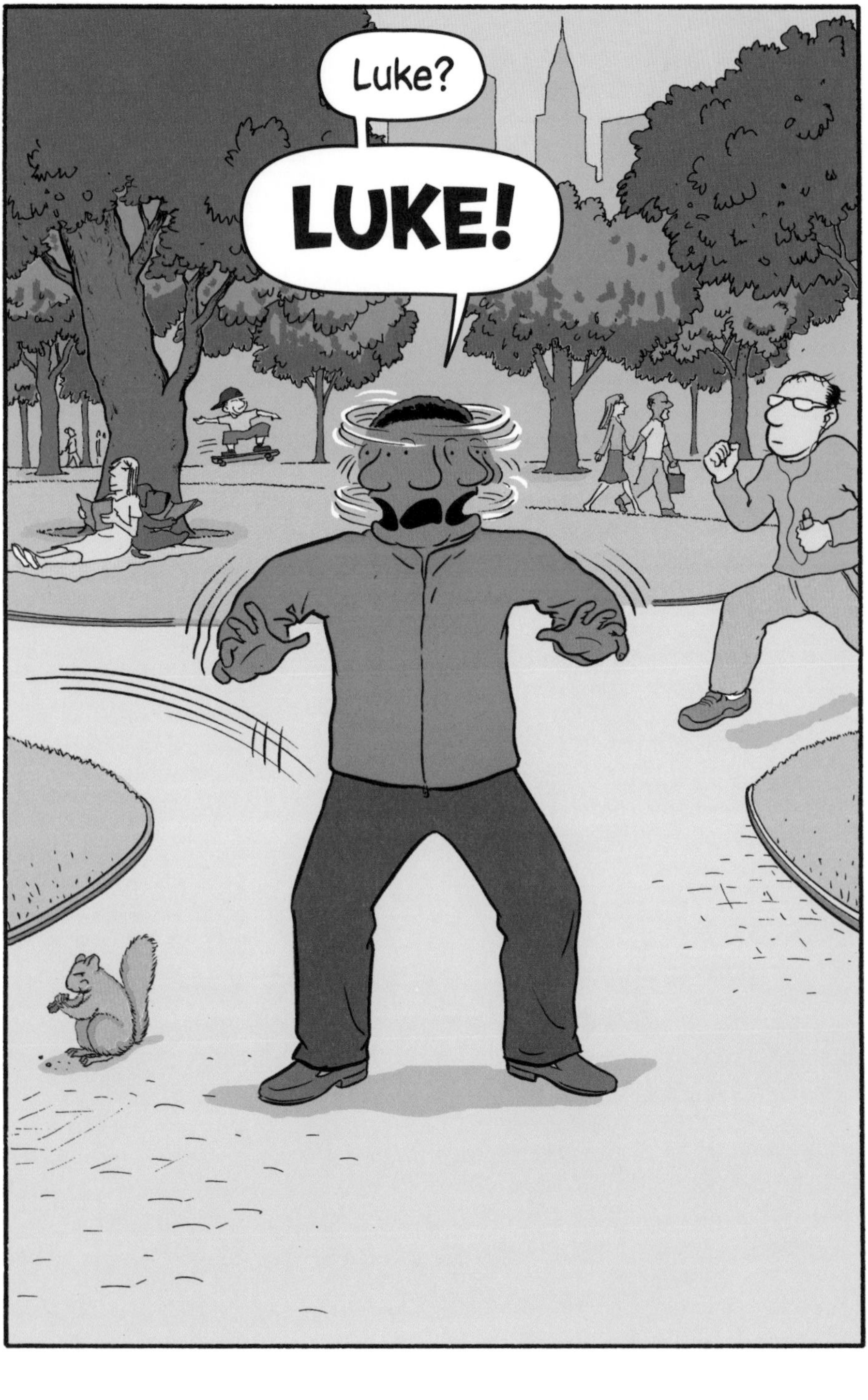
Luke?
LUKE!

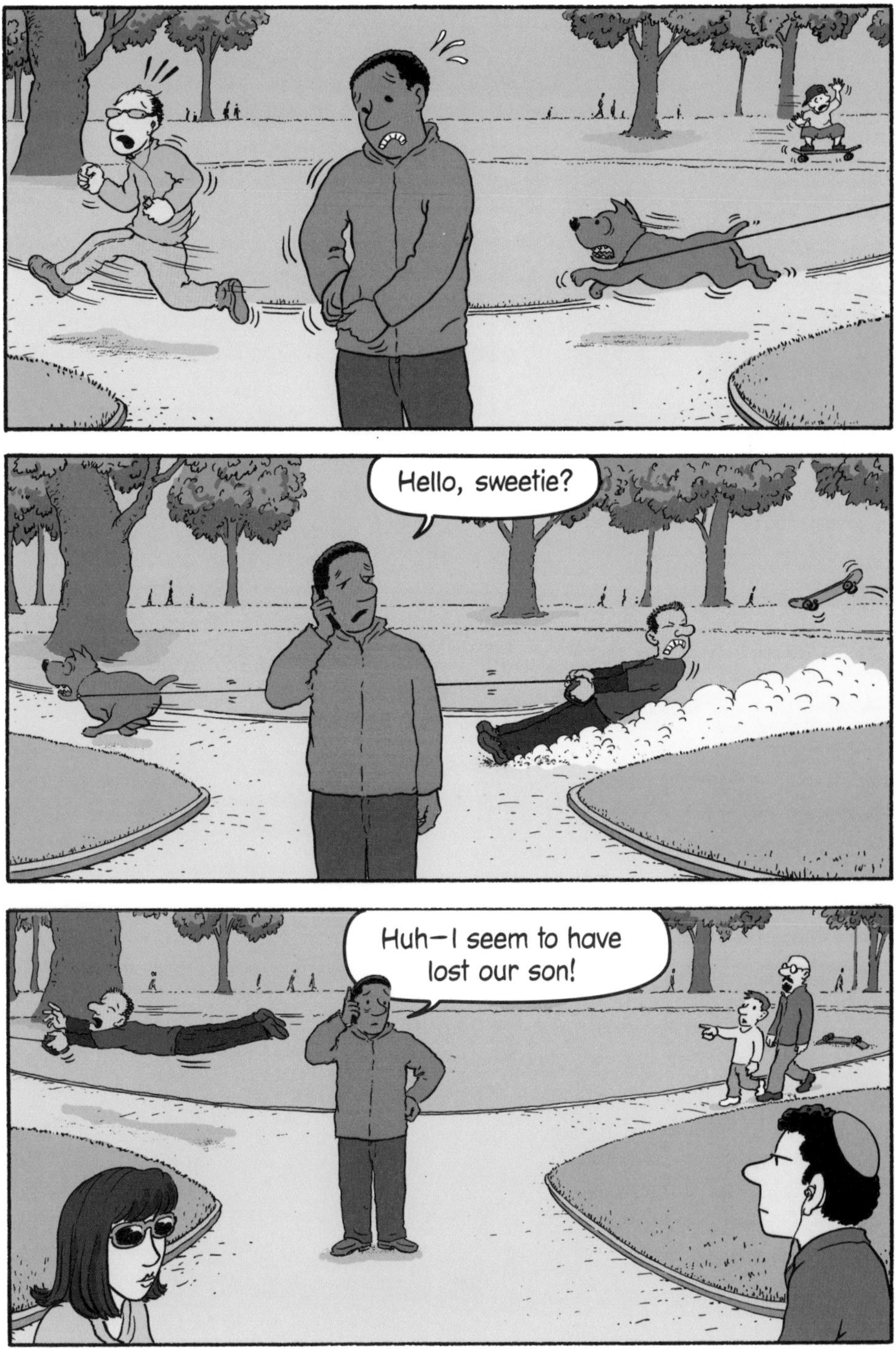
Hello, sweetie?
Huh—I seem to have lost our son!

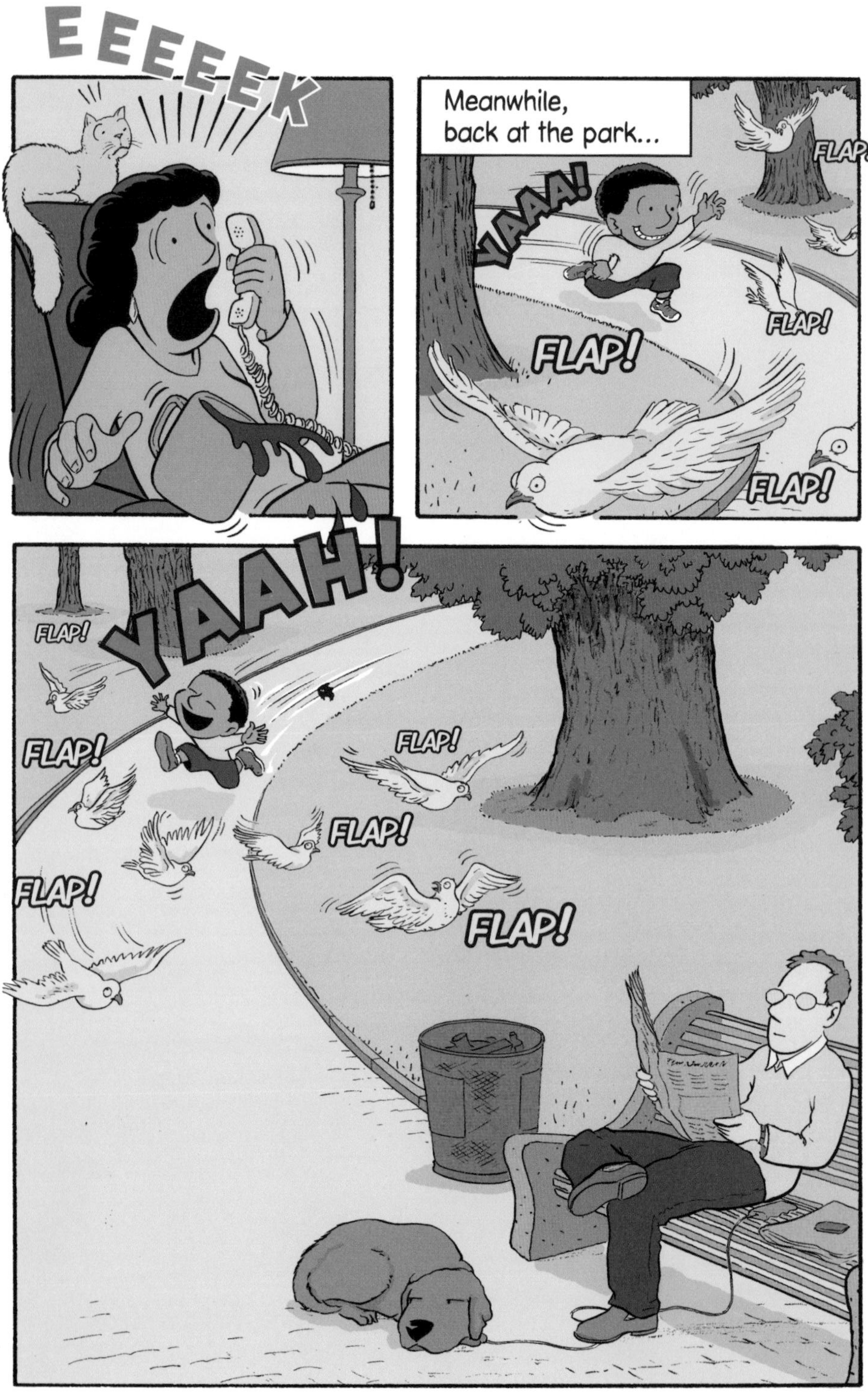
EEEEEK
Meanwhile, back at the park...
YAAAA!
FLAP!
FLAP!
FLAP!
FLAP!
YAAAH!
FLAP!
FLAP!
FLAP!
FLAP!
FLAP!
FLAP!

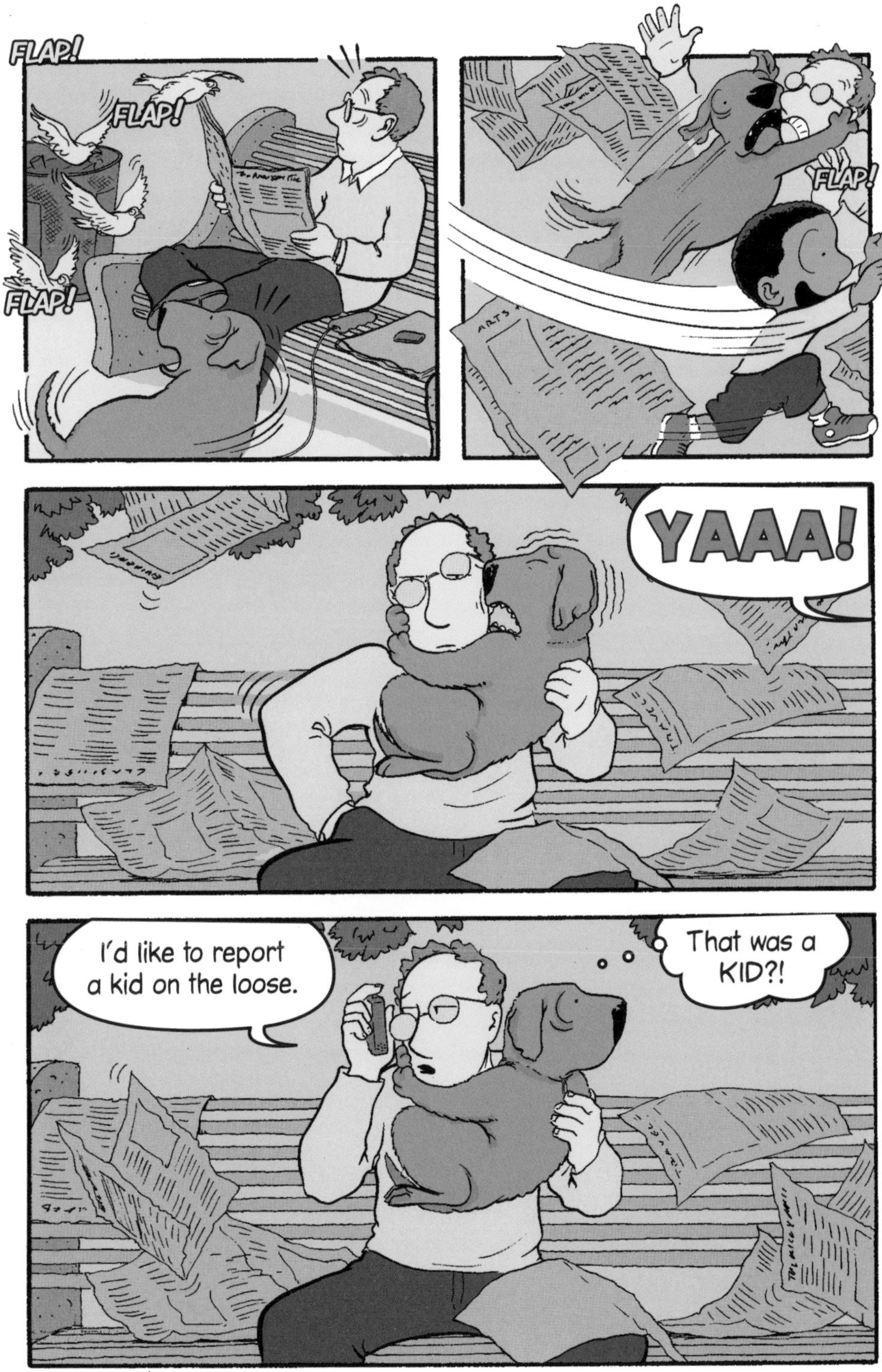
FLAP!
FLAP!
FLAP!
FLAP!
YAAA!
I'd like to report a kid on the loose.
That was a KID?!

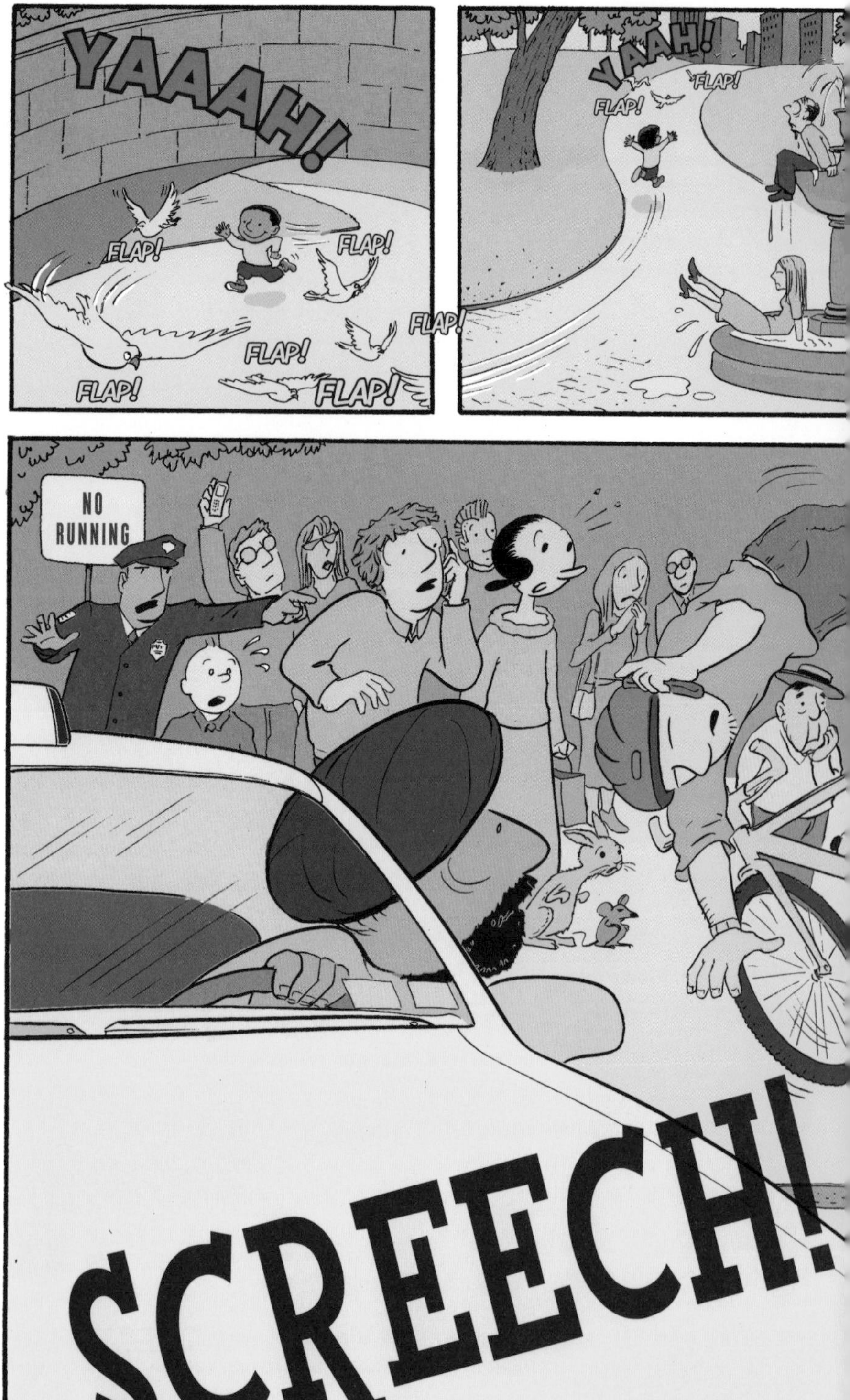
YAAAH!
FLAP!
FLAP!
FLAP!
FLAP!
FLAP!
FLAP!
YAAAH!
FLAP!
FLAP!
NO RUNNING
SCREECH!

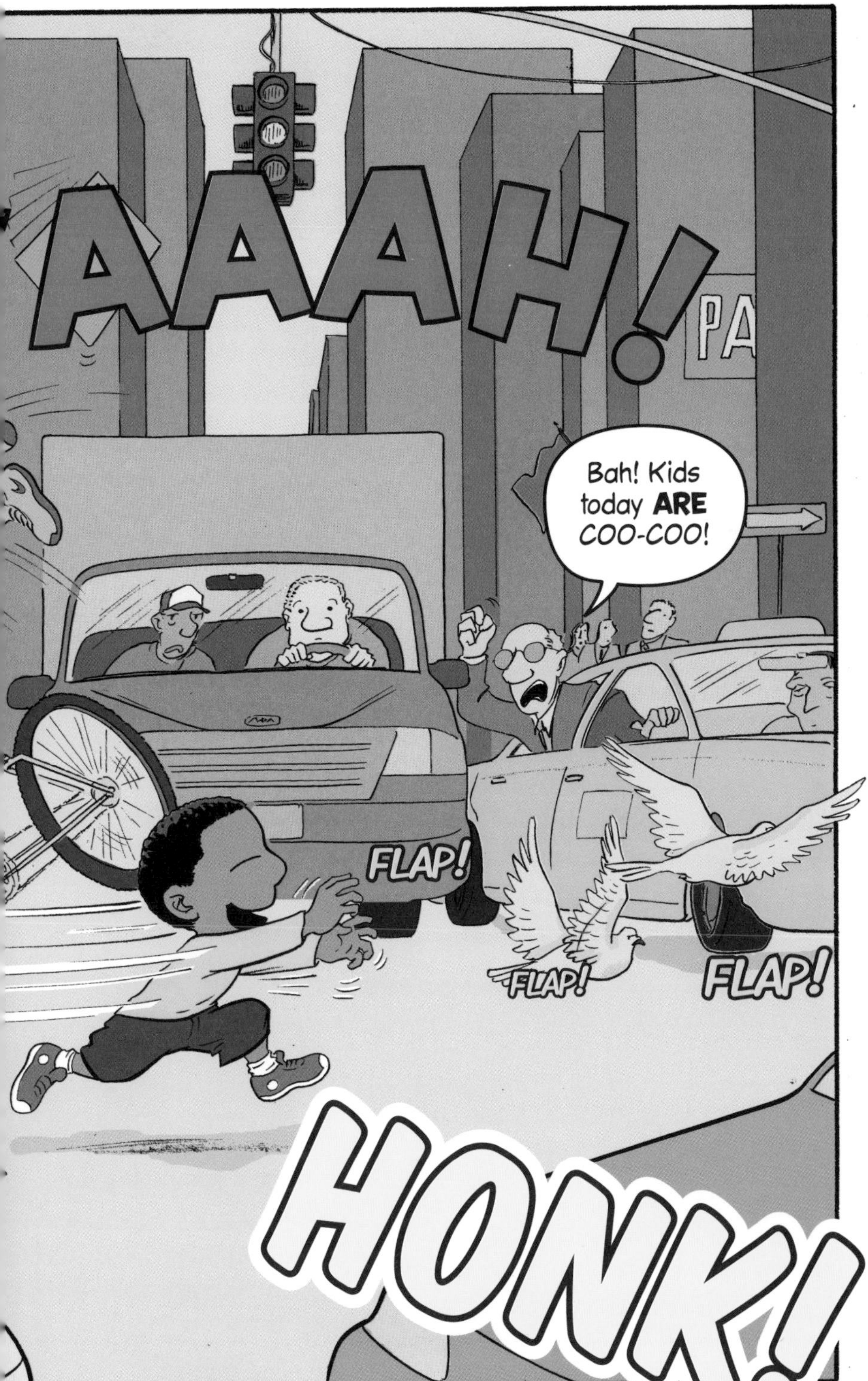
AAAH!
PA
Bah! Kids today **ARE** COO-COO!
FLAP!
FLAP!
FLAP!
HONK!

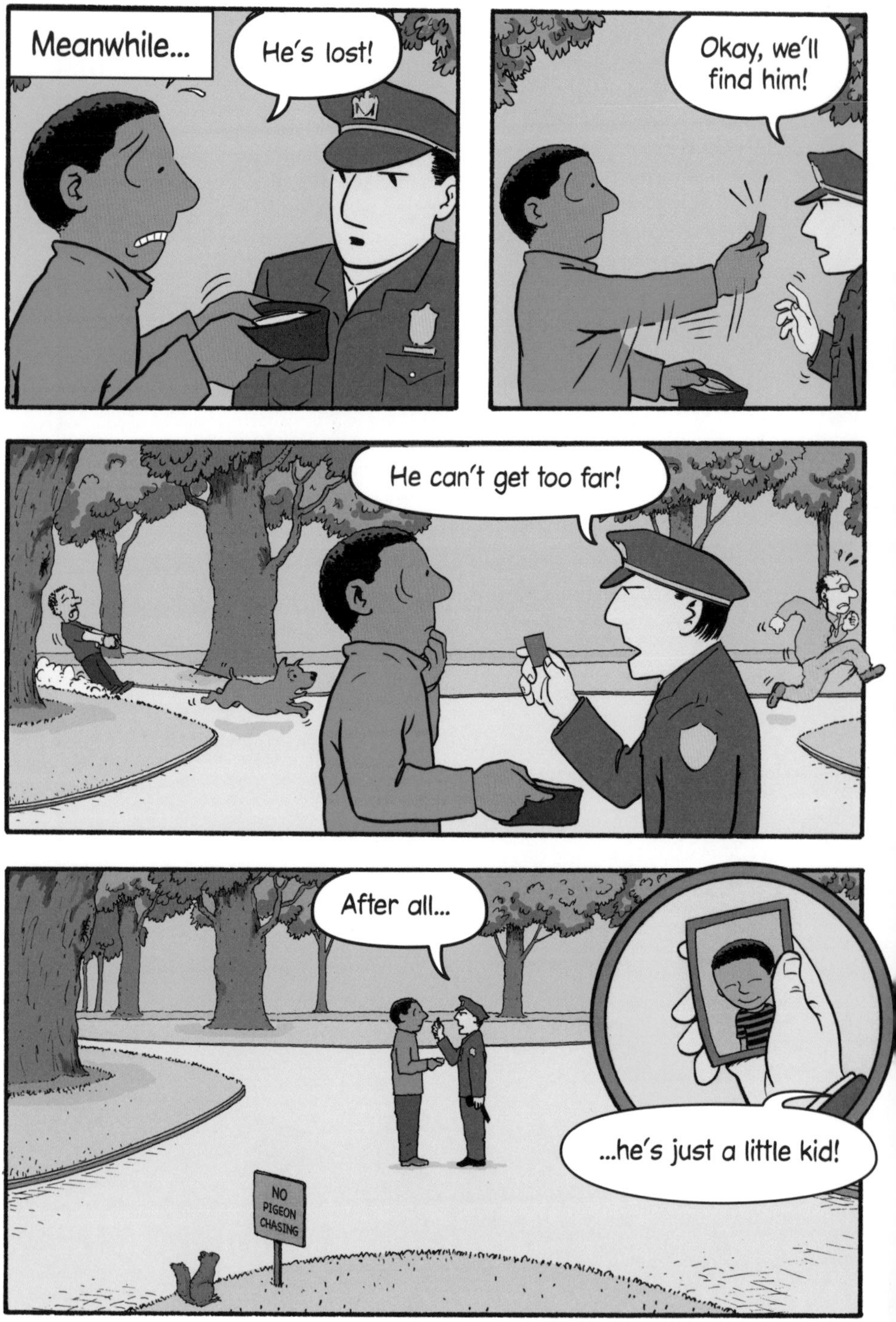
Meanwhile...
He's lost!
Okay, we'll find him!
He can't get too far!
After all...
...he's just a little kid!
NO PIGEON CHASING

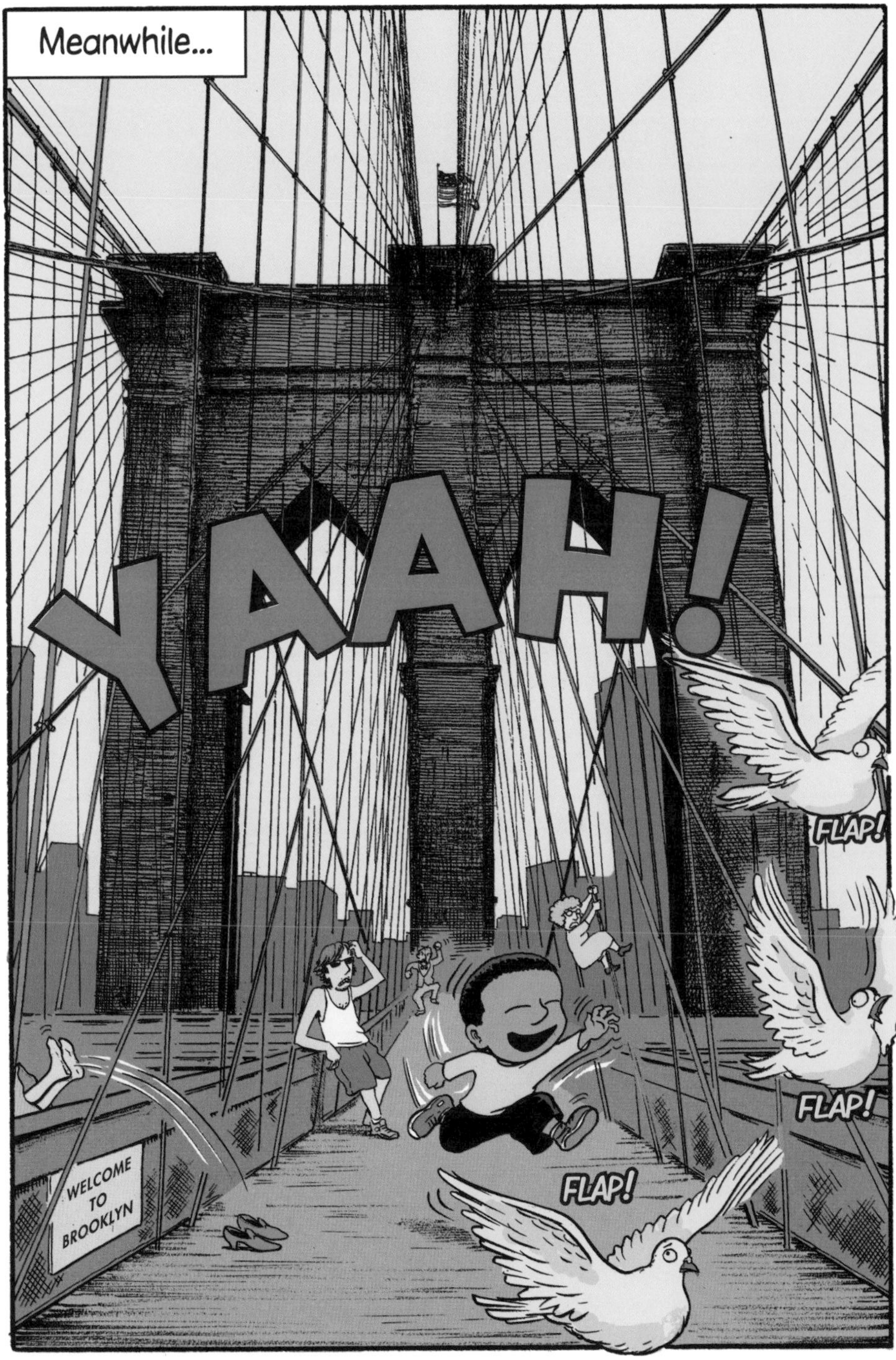
Meanwhile...
YAAH!
FLAP!
FLAP!
FLAP!
WELCOME TO BROOKLYN

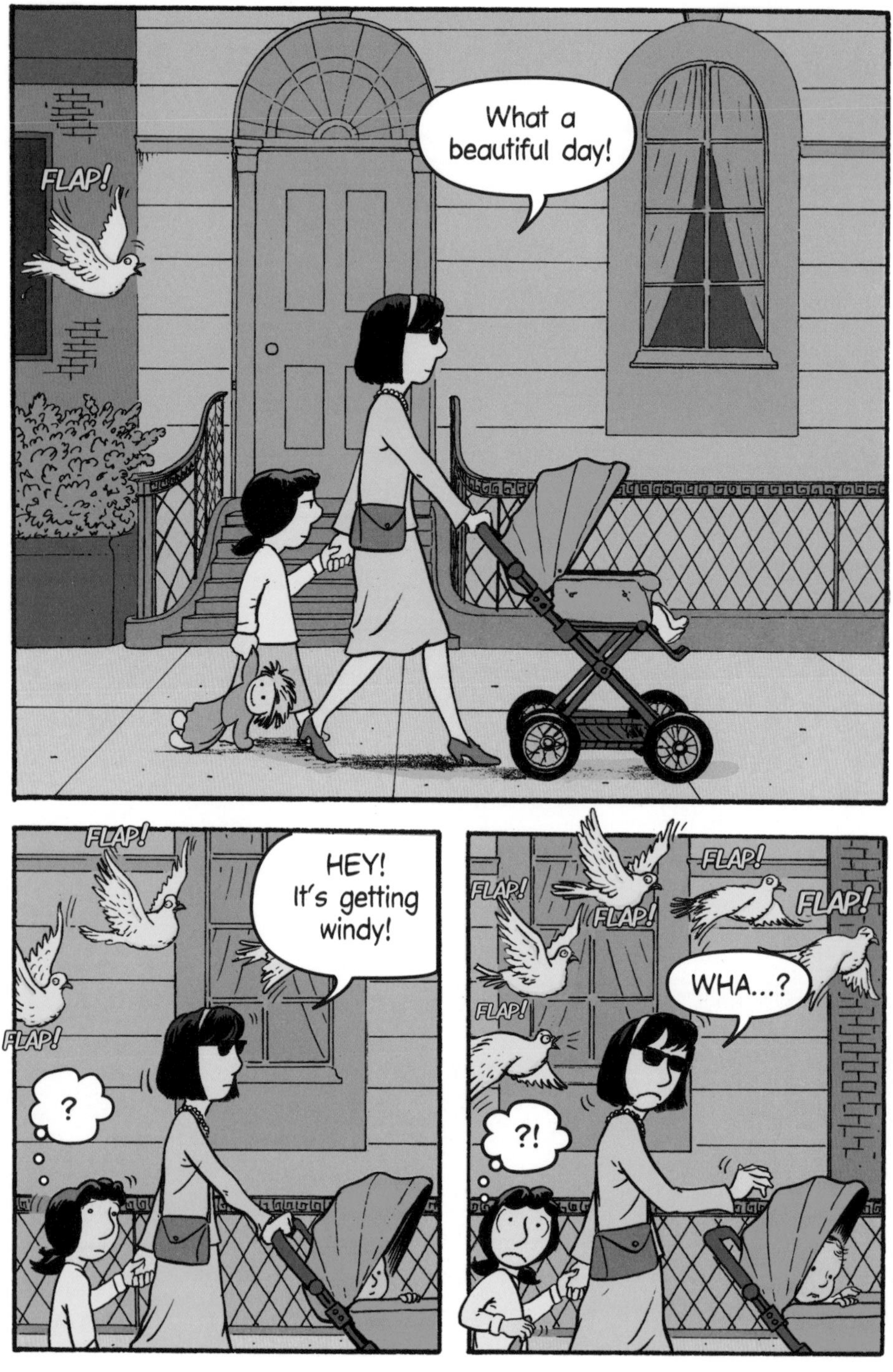
FLAP!
What a beautiful day!
FLAP!
FLAP!
HEY! It's getting windy!
?
FLAP!
FLAP!
FLAP!
FLAP!
FLAP!
WHA...?
?!

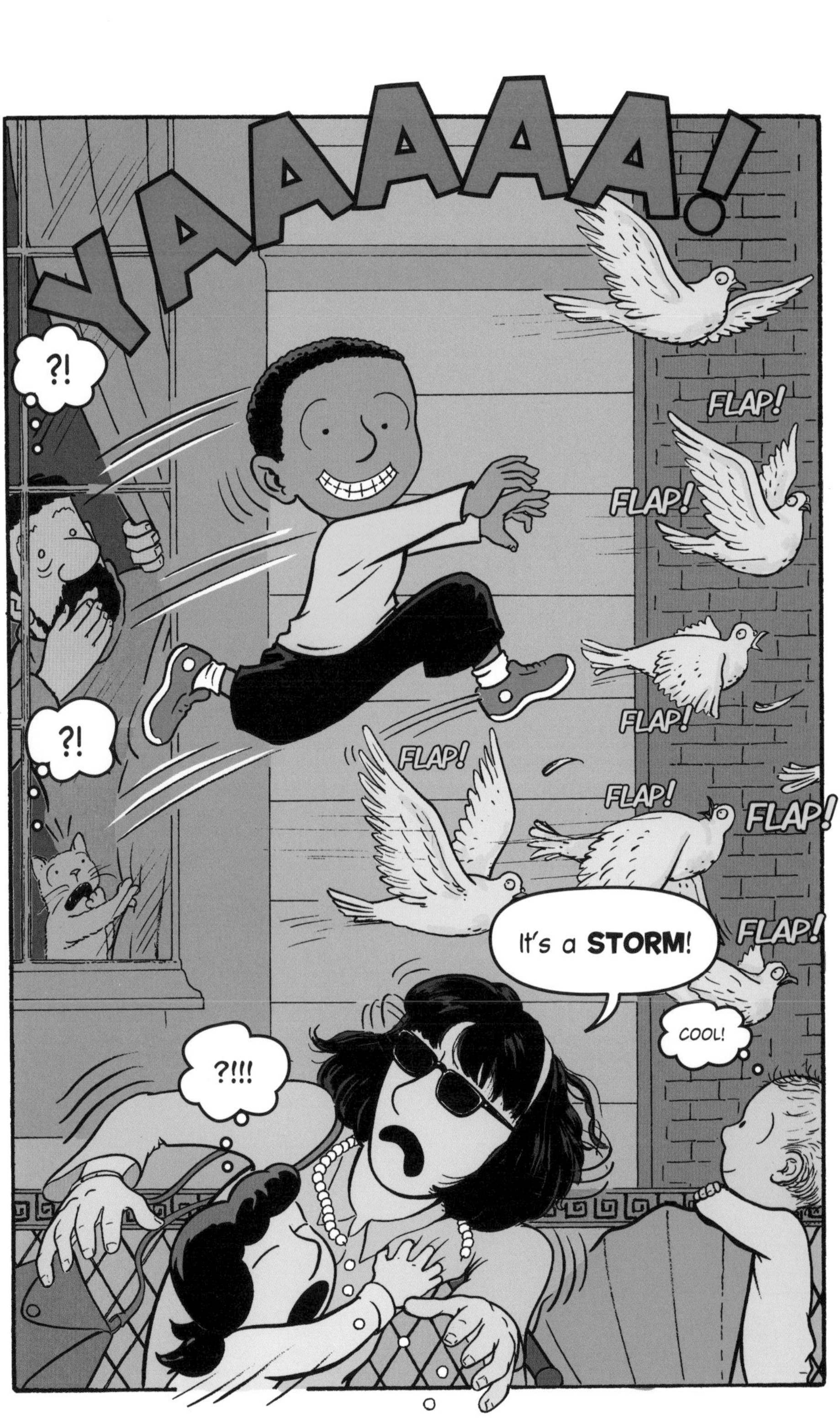
YAAAAA!
?!
FLAP!
FLAP!
?!
FLAP!
FLAP!
FLAP!
FLAP!
It's a **STORM**!
FLAP!
COOL!
?!!!

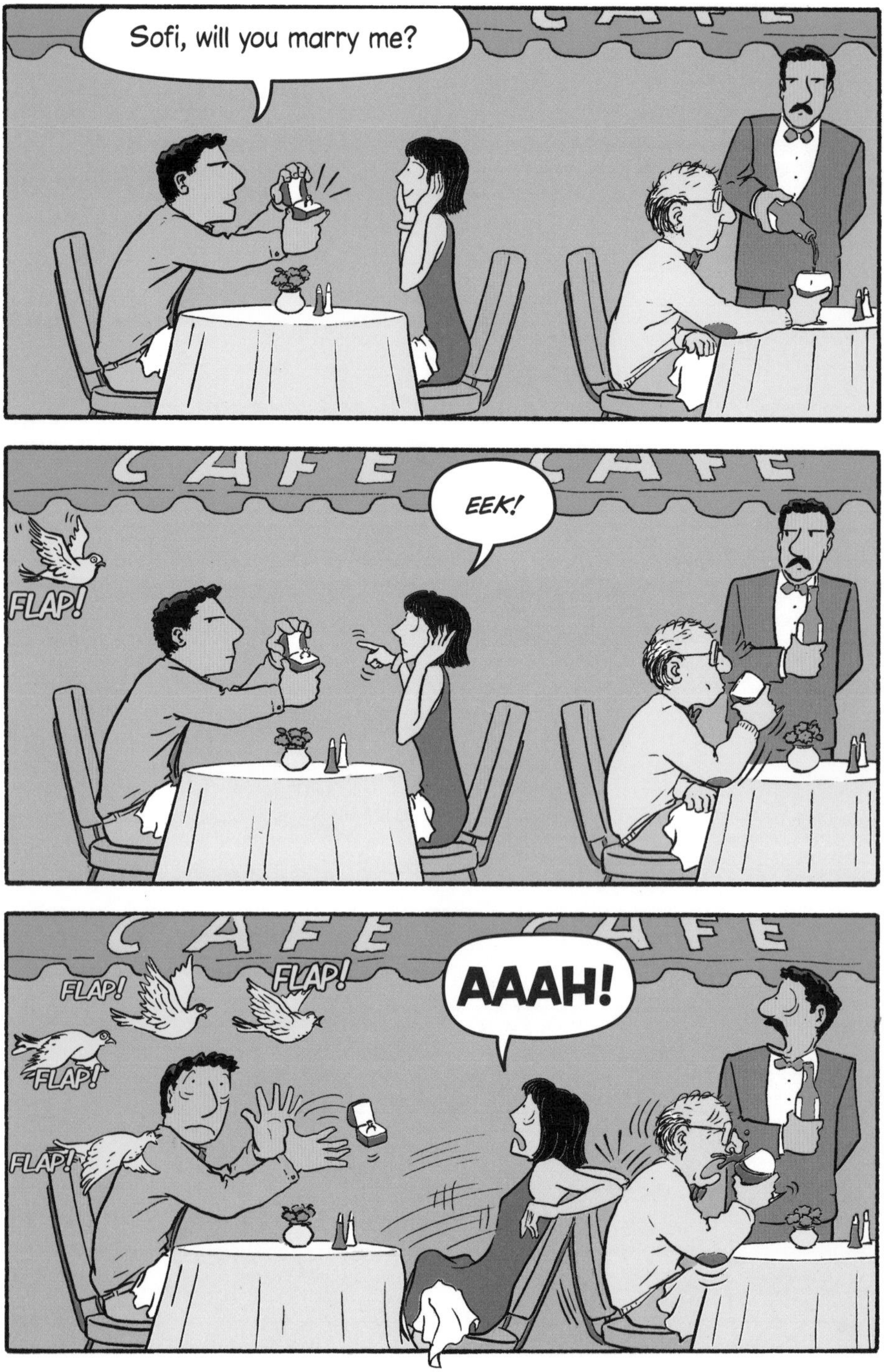
Sofi, will you marry me?
CAFE
EEK!
FLAP!
CAFE CAFE
FLAP!
FLAP!
FLAP!
FLAP!
AAAH!

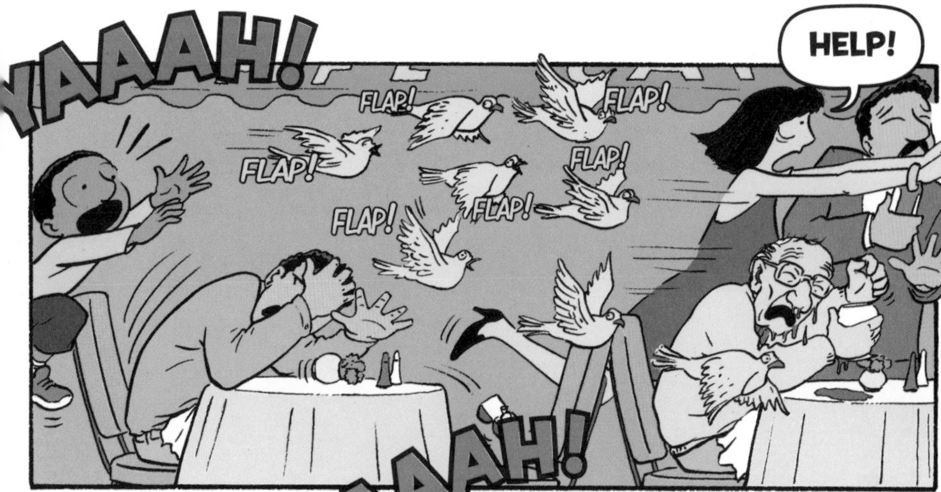
YAAAH!
HELP!
FLAP!
FLAP!
FLAP!
FLAP!
FLAP!
FLAP!
YAAAH!

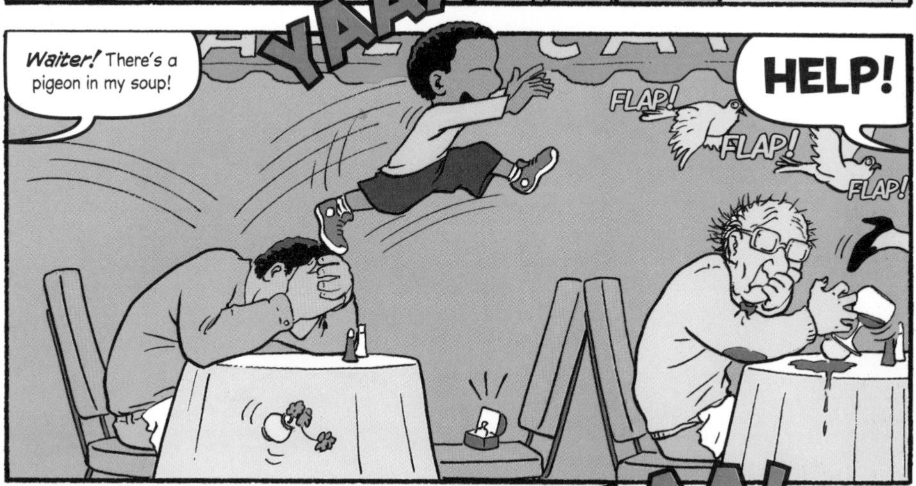
YAAAH!
Waiter! There's a pigeon in my soup!
HELP!
FLAP!
FLAP!
FLAP!

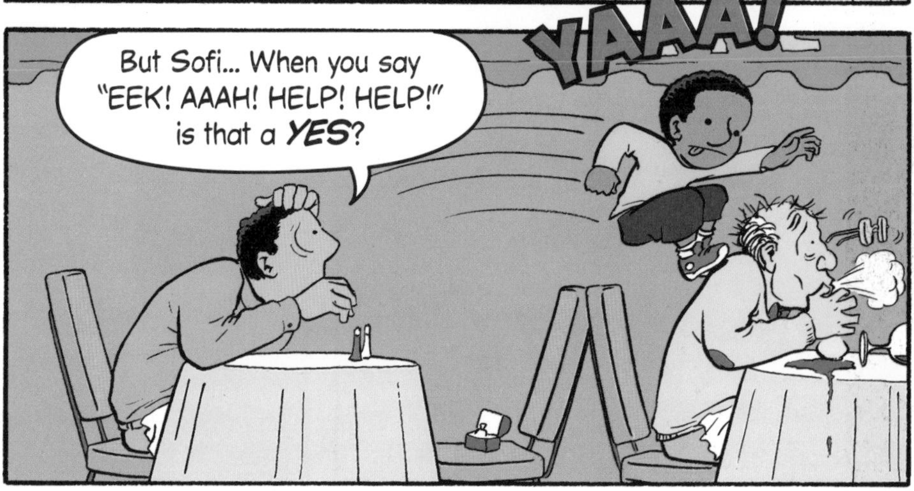
YAAA!
But Sofi... When you say "EEK! AAAH! HELP! HELP!" is that a ***YES***?

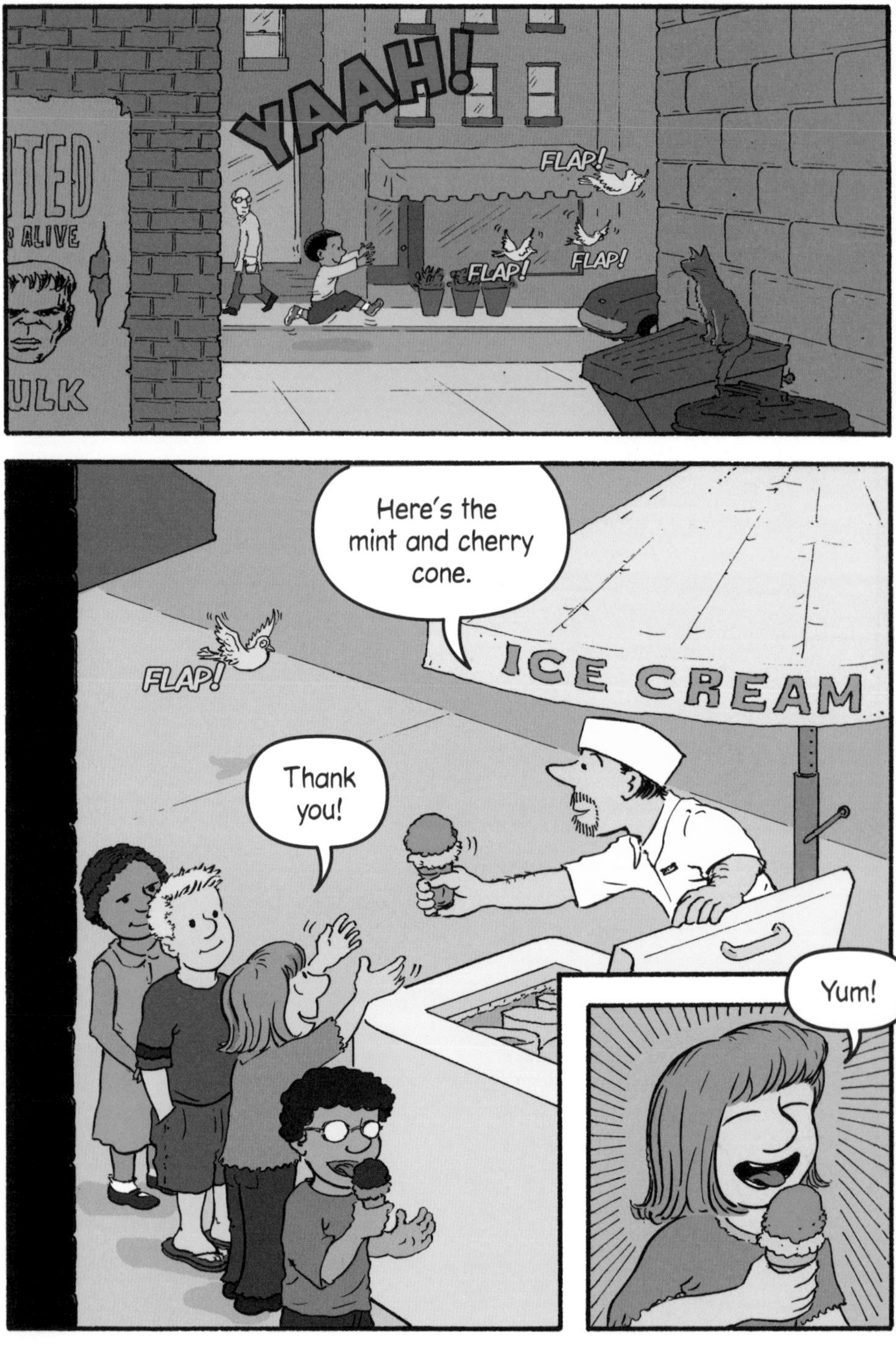
TED
R ALIVE
ULK
YAAAH!
FLAP!
FLAP!
FLAP!
Here's the mint and cherry cone.
FLAP!
ICE CREAM
Thank you!
Yum!

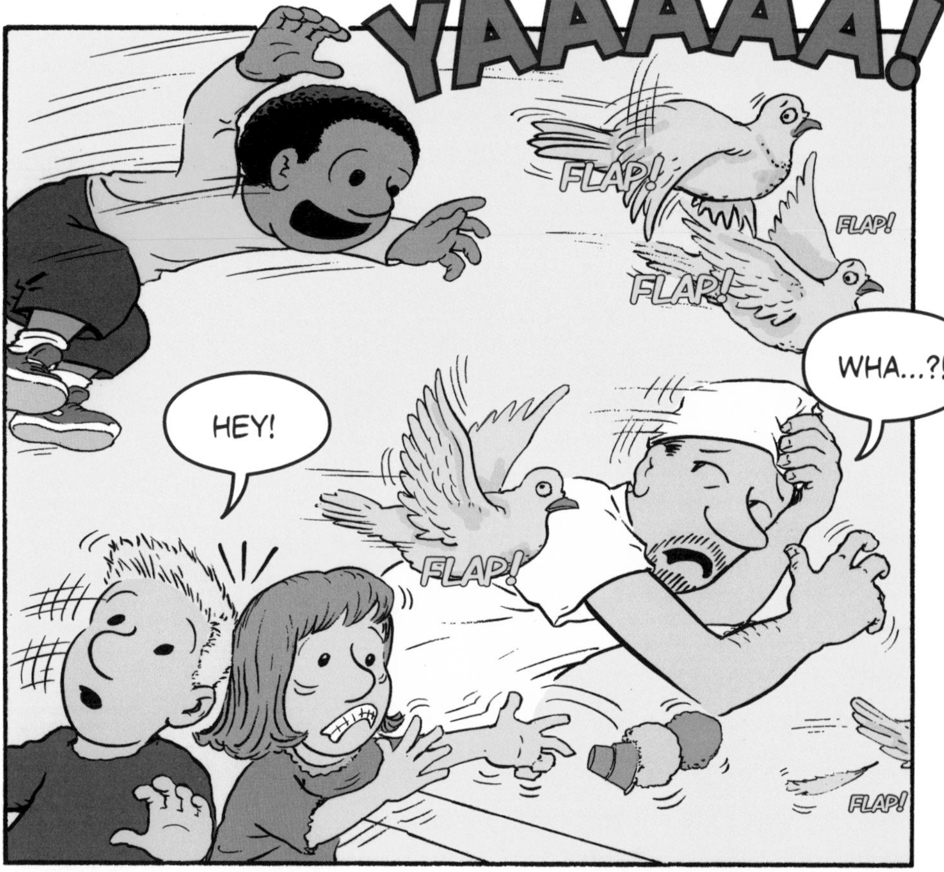
YAAAAA!
FLAP!
FLAP!
FLAP!
WHA...?!
HEY!
FLAP!
FLAP!

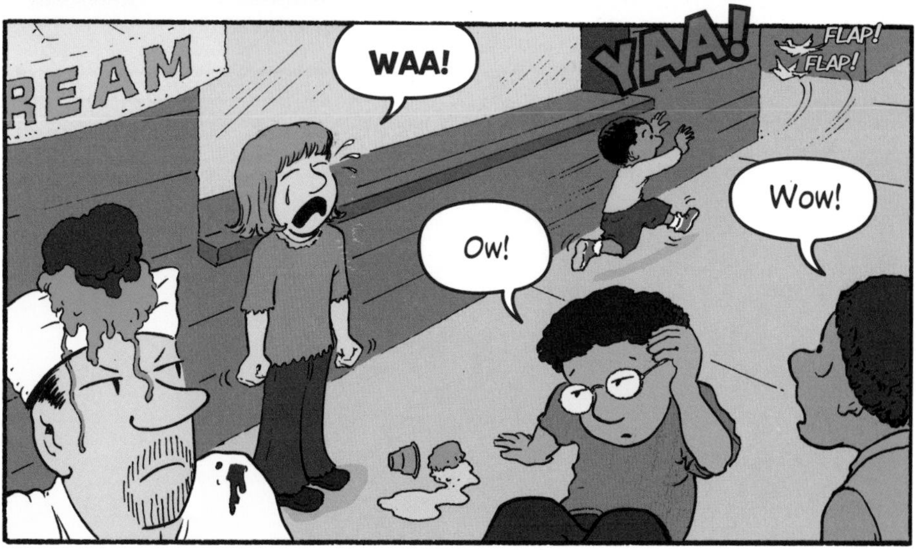
REAM
WAA!
YAA!
FLAP!
FLAP!
Wow!
Ow!

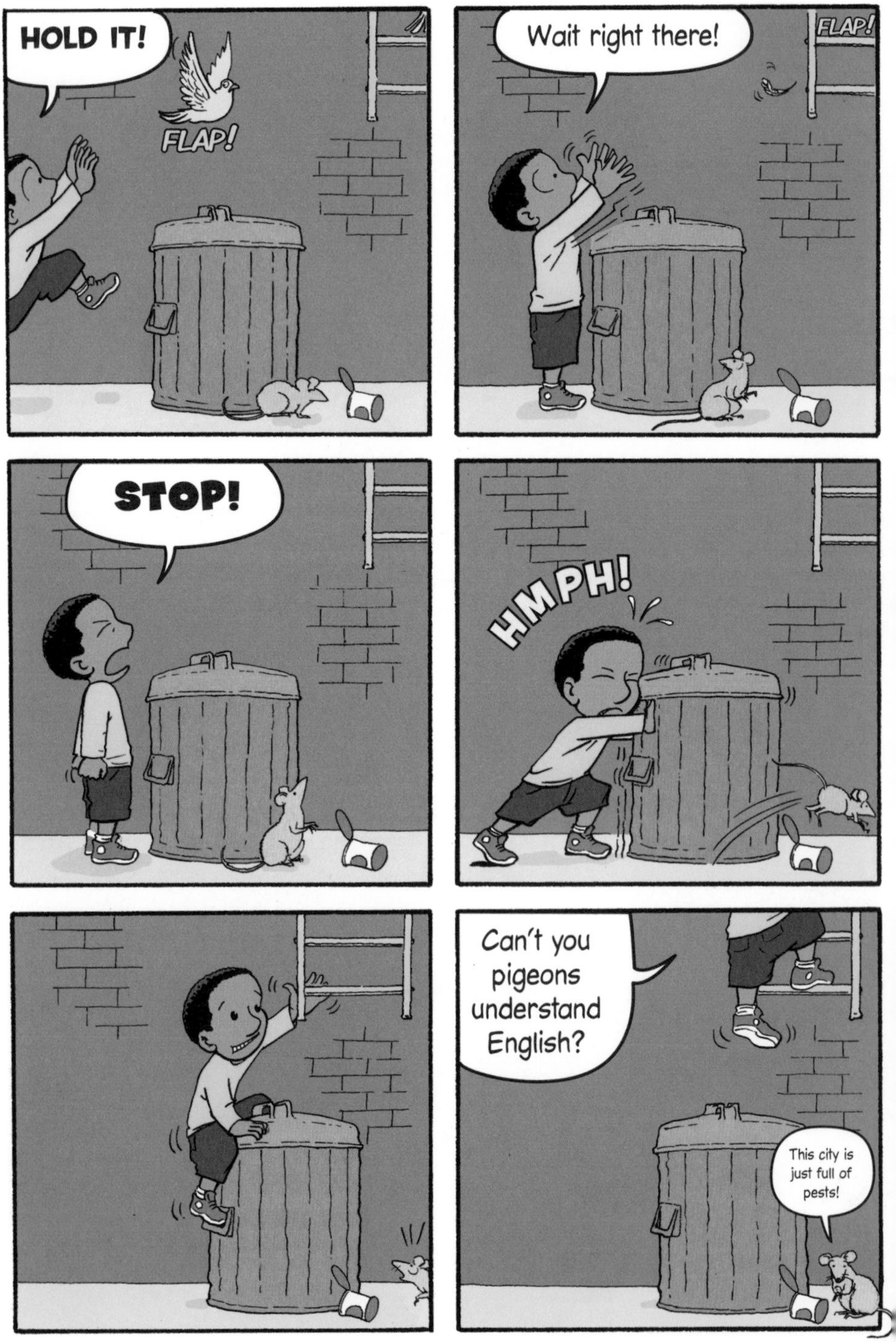
HOLD IT!
FLAP!
Wait right there!
FLAP!
STOP!
HMPH!
Can't you pigeons understand English?
This city is just full of pests!

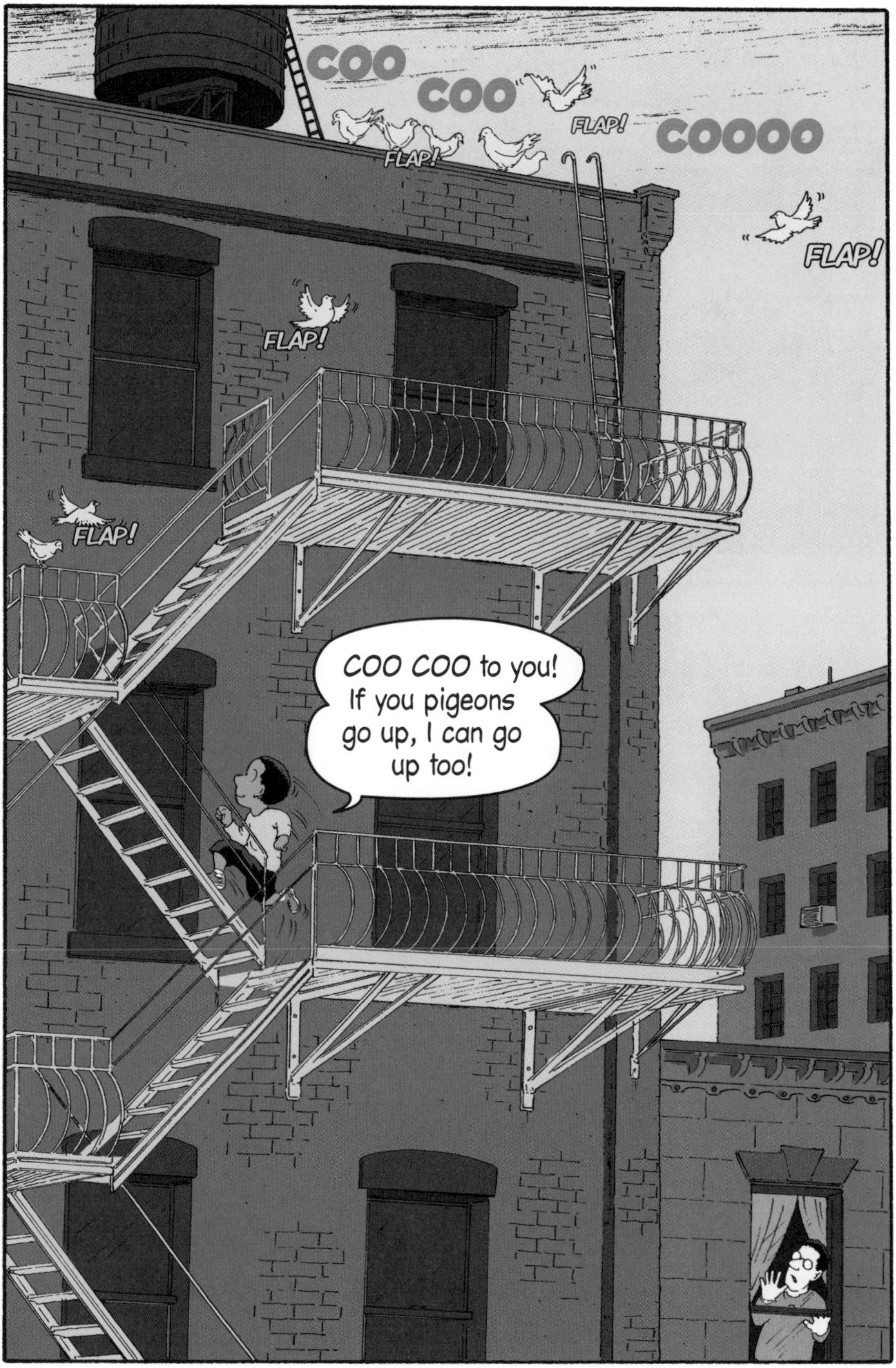
COO
COO
FLAP!
FLAP!
COOOO
FLAP!
FLAP!
FLAP!
COO COO to you! If you pigeons go up, I can go up too!

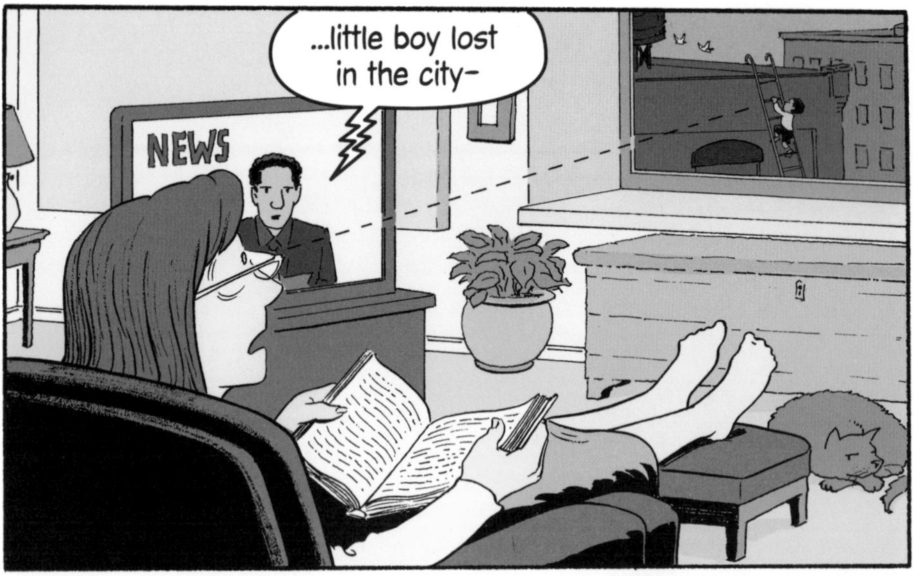
...little boy lost in the city-
NEWS

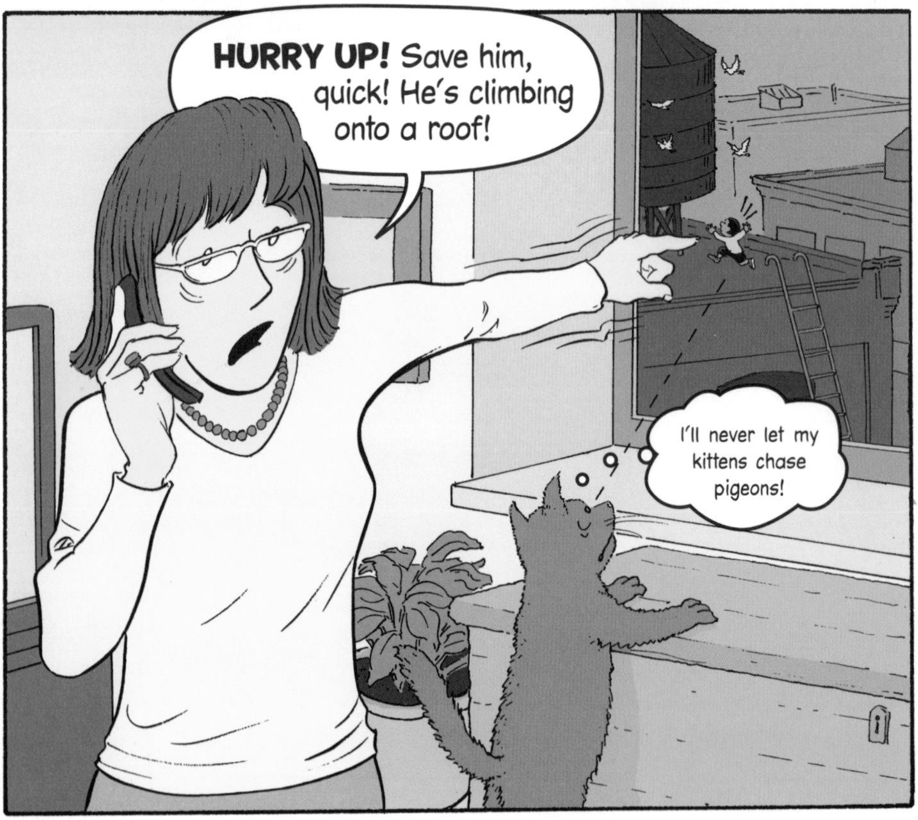
HURRY UP! Save him, quick! He's climbing onto a roof!
I'll never let my kittens chase pigeons!

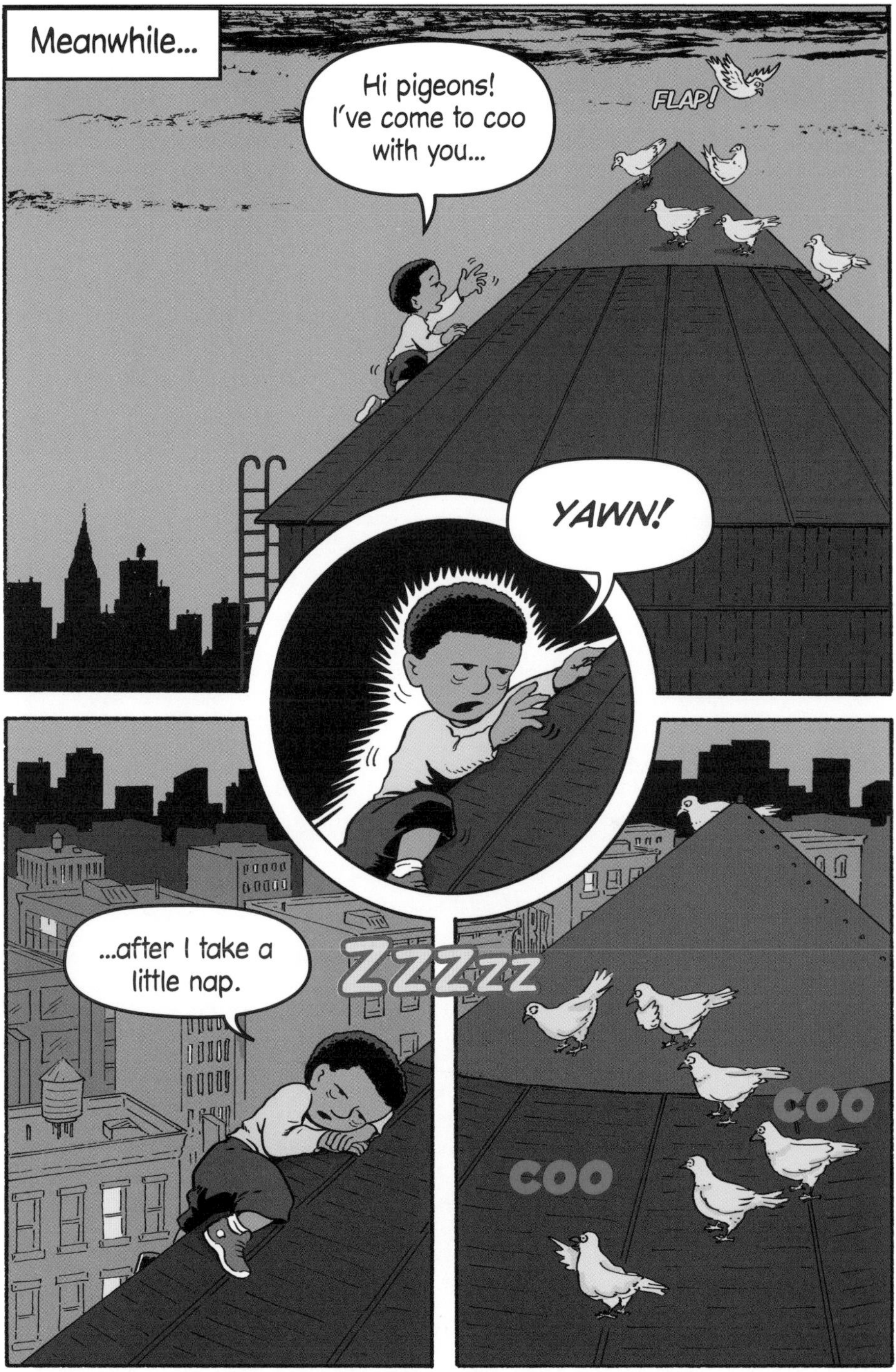
Meanwhile...
Hi pigeons! I've come to coo with you...
FLAP!
YAWN!
...after I take a little nap.
ZZZzz
COO
COO

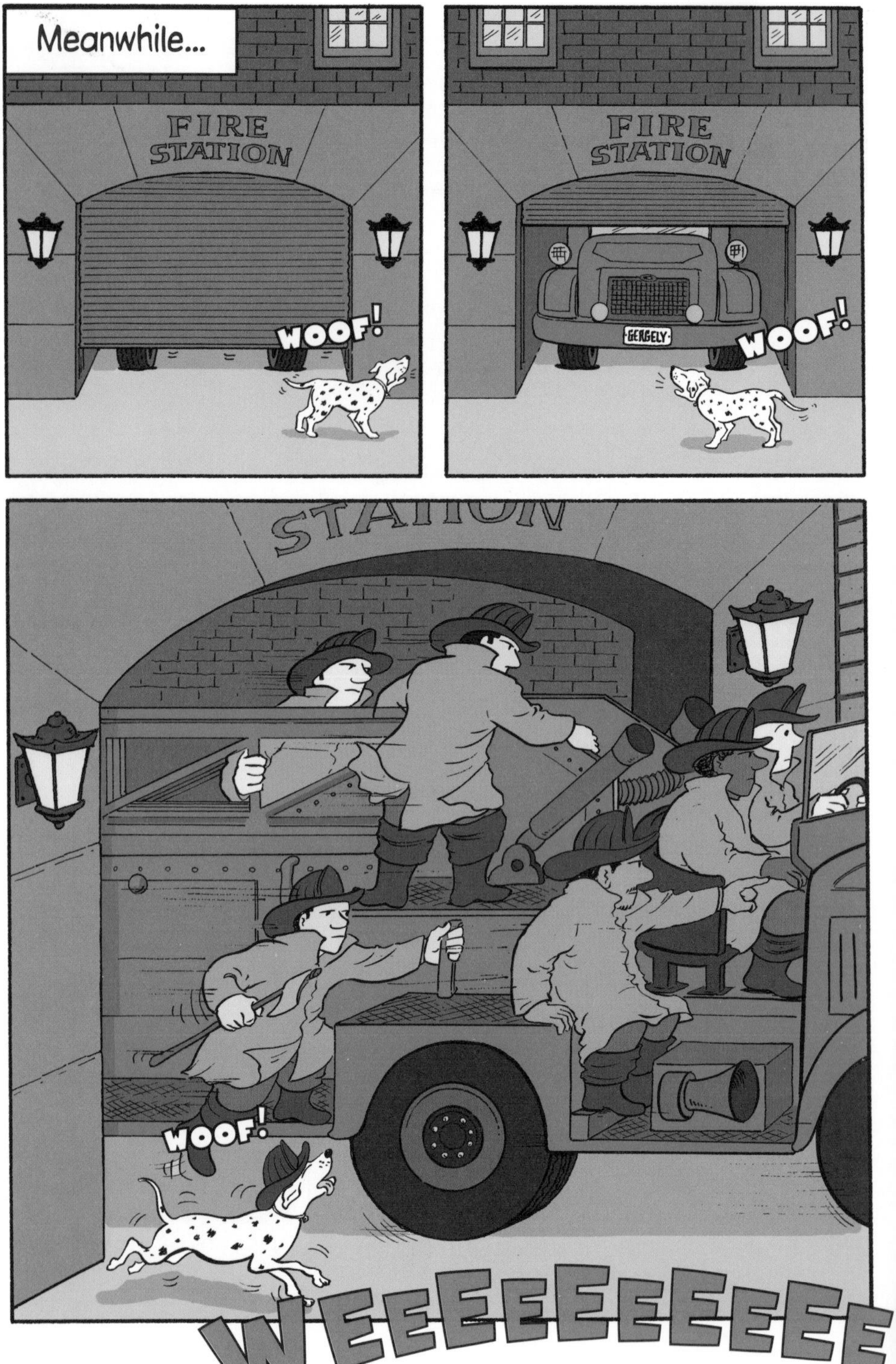
Meanwhile...
FIRE STATION
WOOF!
FIRE STATION
GERGELY
WOOF!
STATION
WOOF!
WEEEEEEEEEE

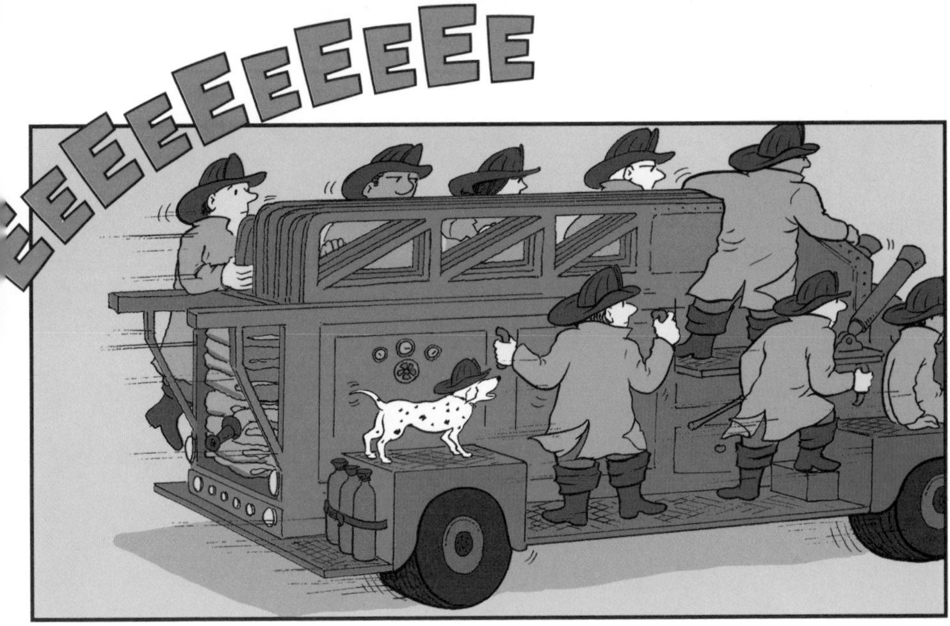
EEEEEEEEEEEE

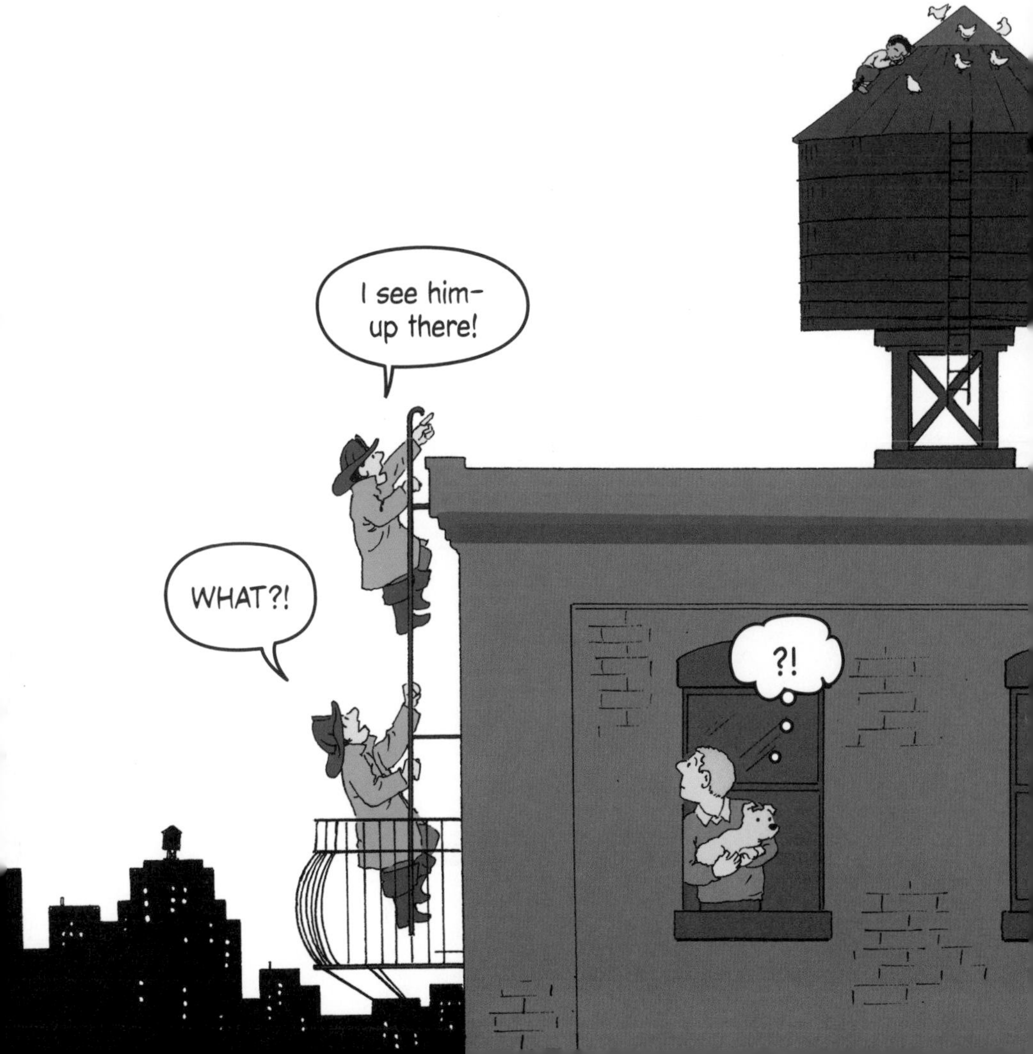
I see him-
up there!
WHAT?!
?!

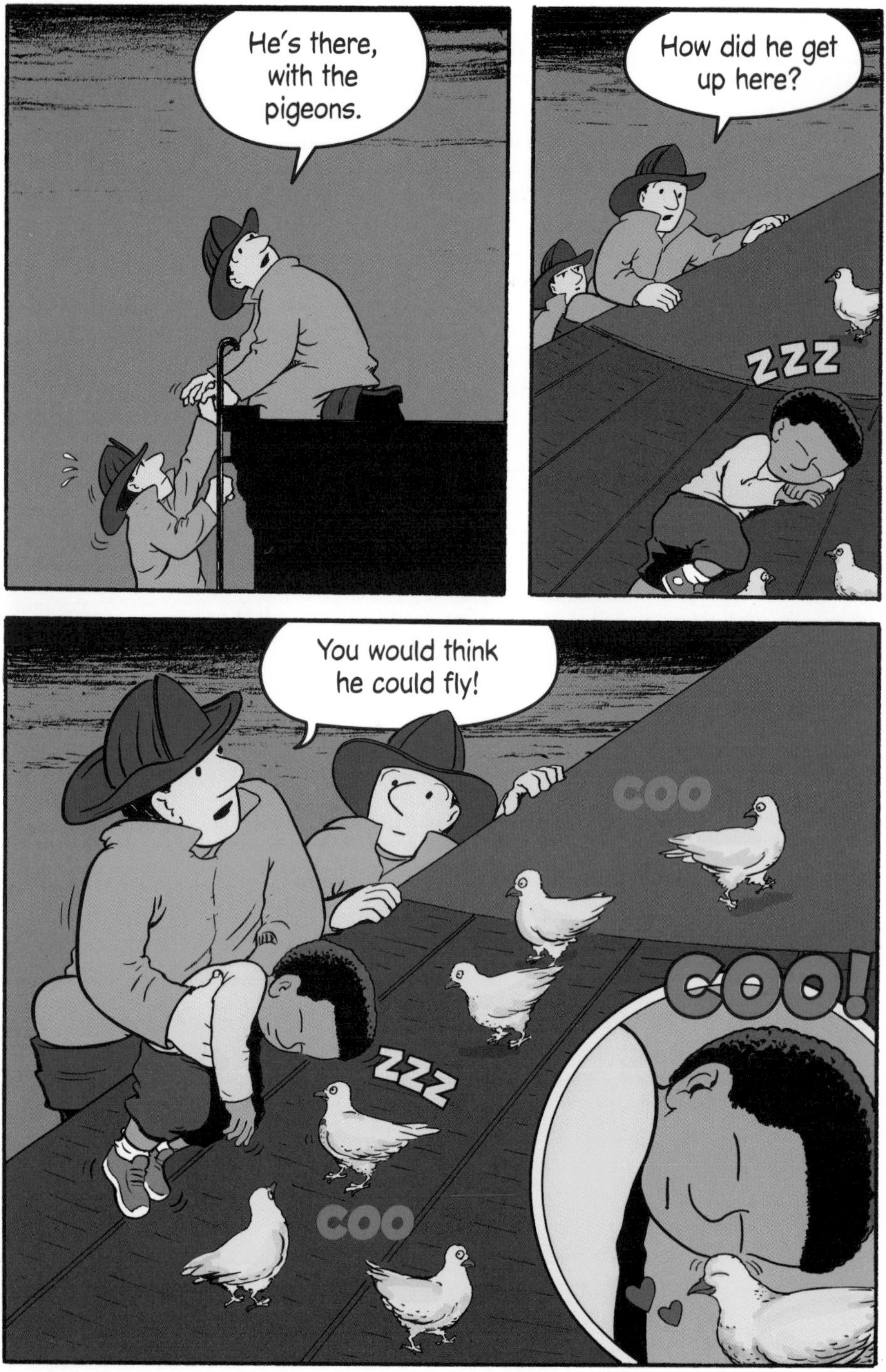
He's there, with the pigeons.
How did he get up here?
ZZZ
You would think he could fly!
COO
COO!
ZZZ
COO

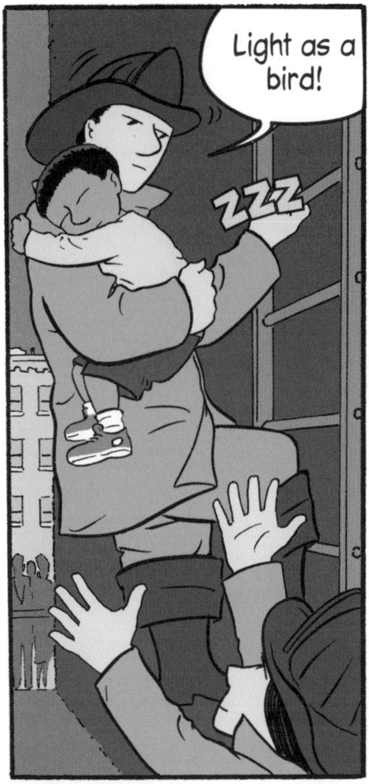
Light as a bird!
ZZZ
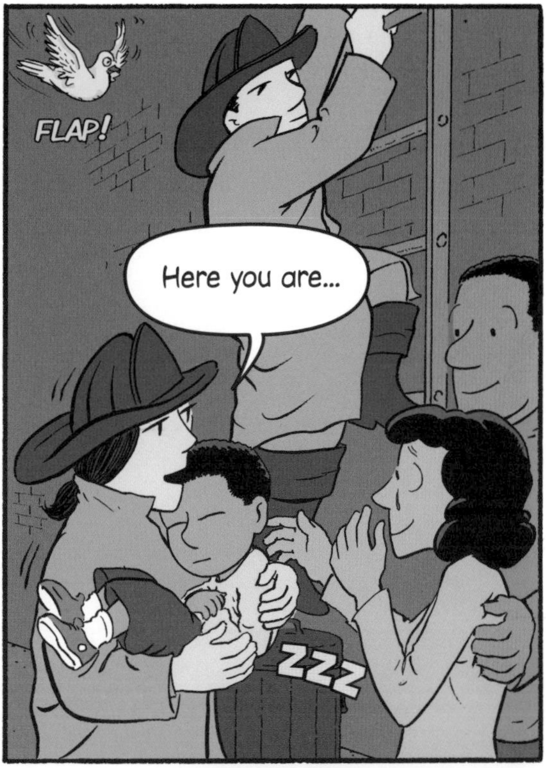
FLAP!
Here you are...
ZZZ
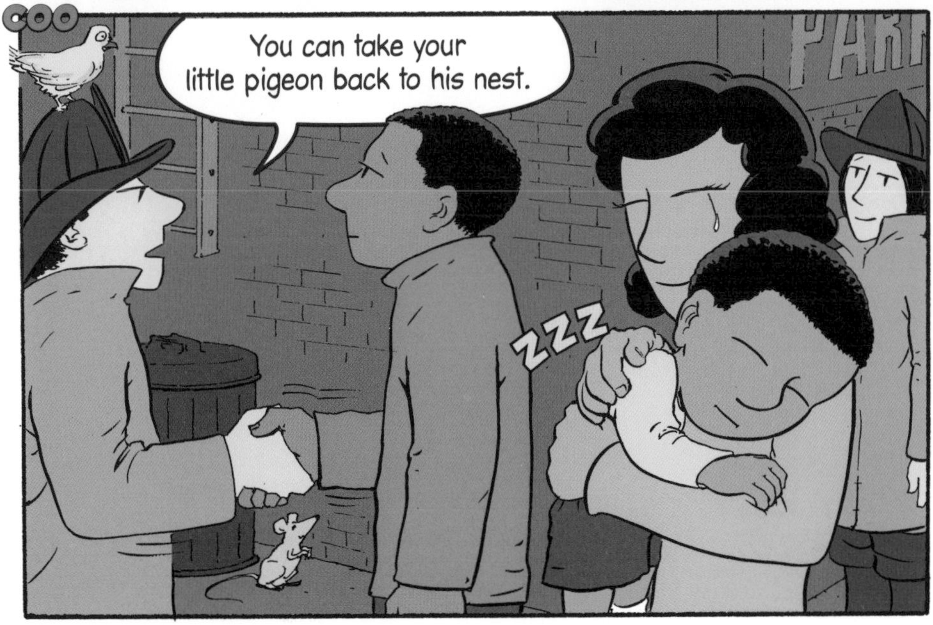
COO
You can take your little pigeon back to his nest.
ZZZ

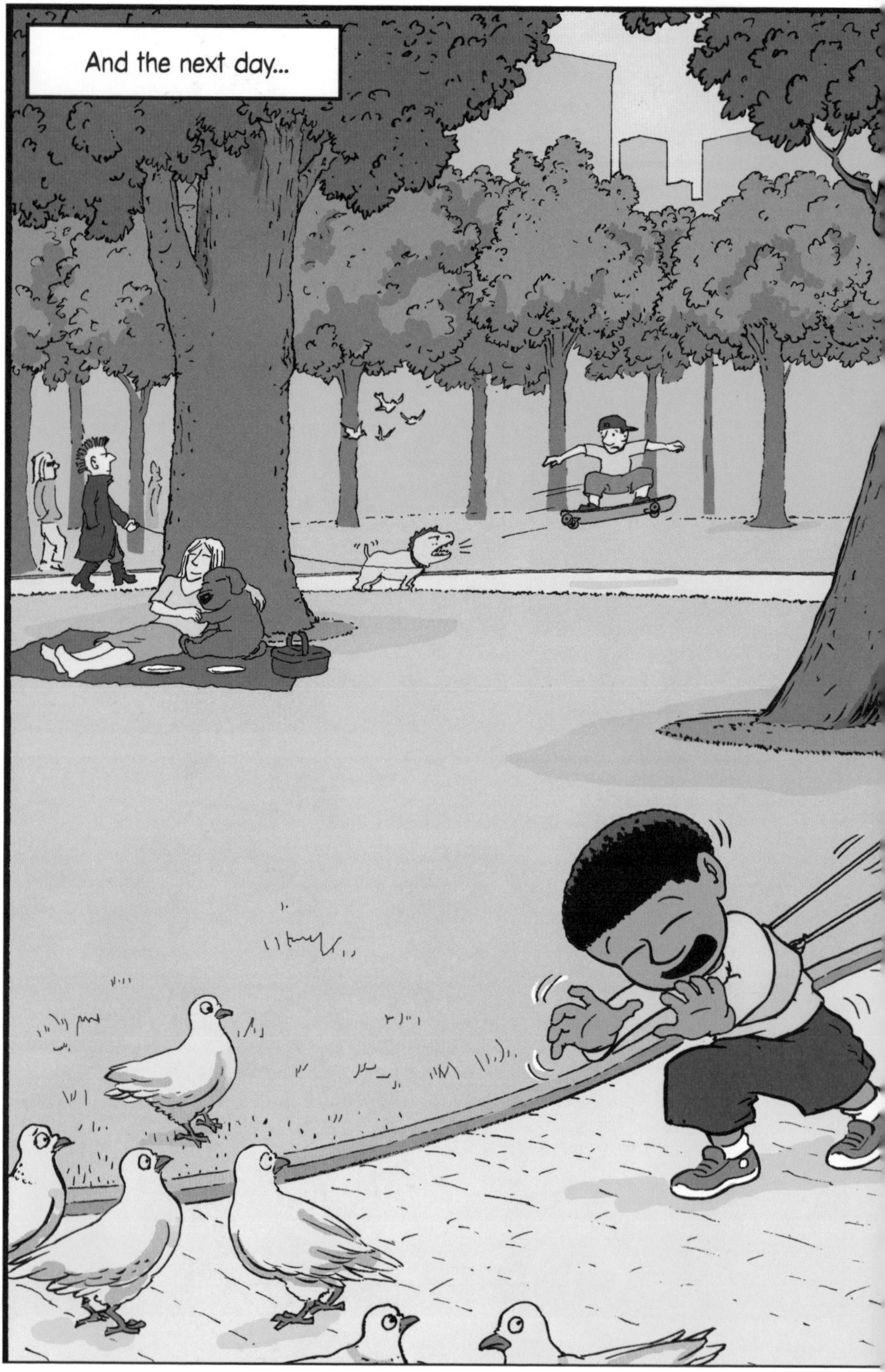
And the next day...

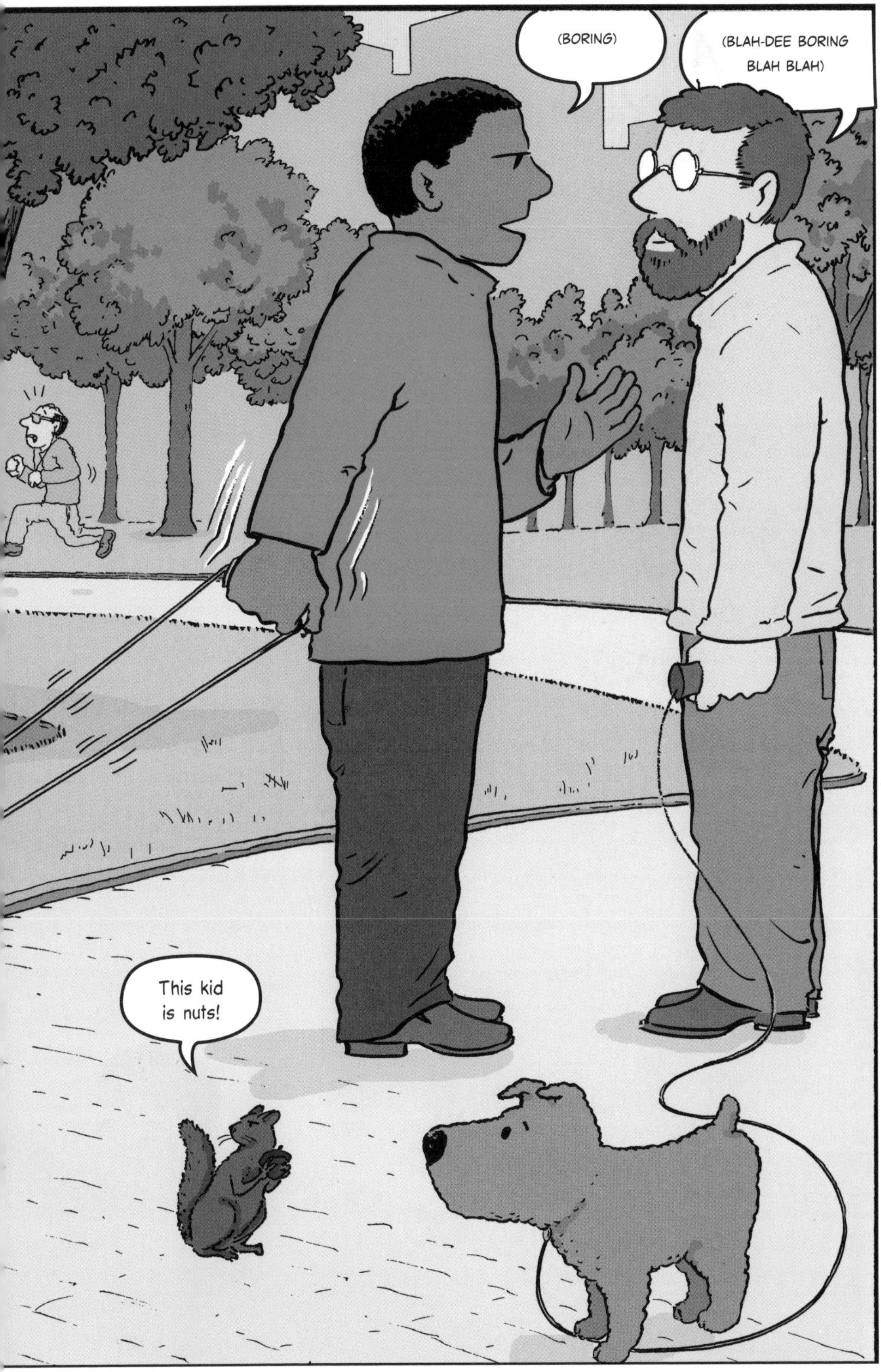
(BORING)
(BLAH-DEE BORING BLAH BLAH)
This kid is nuts!

THE END

ABOUT THE AUTHOR

HARRY BLISS never chased pigeons. He grew up in upstate New York, often staying up late at night and laughing himself to sleep while looking at Will Elder's *MAD Magazine* drawings. He dreamt of a life in a New York City as zany as a Will Elder panel and was perpetually late for his school bus. Harry is now a beloved *New Yorker* cartoonist and cover artist as well as the illustrator of numerous best-selling children's books. Many of his books, such as *A Fine, Fine School,* by Sharon Creech, and *Diary of a Worm, Diary of a Fly,* and *Diary of a Spider,* by Doreen Cronin, have become children's favorites. He also illustrated *Which Would You Rather Be?* by Caldecott Medal-winner William Steig, and *Louise, The Adventures of a Chicken* by Newbery Medal-winner Kate DiCamillo. This is his first comic book story.

Harry currently lives in northern Vermont with his son and their puppy, Penny; Penny has yet to catch her first squirrel.

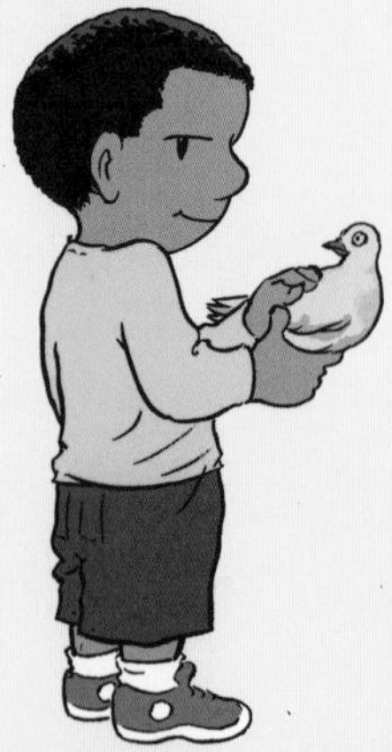

HOW TO "TOON INTO READING"

in a few simple steps:

Our goal is to get kids reading—and we know kids LOVE comics. We publish award-winning early readers in comics form on three levels for elementary and early middle school.

1 FIND THE RIGHT BOOK

Veteran teacher Cindy Rosado tells what makes a good book for beginning and struggling readers alike: "A vetted vocabulary, plenty of picture clues, repetition, and a clear and compelling story. Also, the book shouldn't be too easy—or the reader won't learn, but neither should it be too hard—or he or she may get discouraged."

The TOON INTO READING!™ program is designed for beginning readers and works wonders with reluctant readers.

MO AND JO
FIGHTING TOGETHER FOREVER
BENJAMIN BEAR
in Fuzzy Thinking
ZIG AND WIKKI
SOMETHING ATE MY HOMEWORK
NADJA SPIEGELMAN & TRADE LOEFFLER
BENNY AND PENNY
THE BIG NO-NO!
Oh, Benny, this is a very big NO-NO!
Yes!
GEOFFREY HAYES
CHICK & CHICKIE
PLAY ALL DAY!
What do you want to play?
Claude Ponti
Little Mouse Gets Ready
THAT'S ME!
Jeff Smith
THE SHARK KING

2 TAKE TIME WITH SILENT PANELS

Comics use panels to mark time, and silent panels count. Look and "read" even when there are no words. Often, humor is all in the timing!

KNOCK! KNOCK!
TRICK OR TREAT!

What works?
Keep your fingertip below the character that is speaking.

3 GUIDE YOUNG READERS

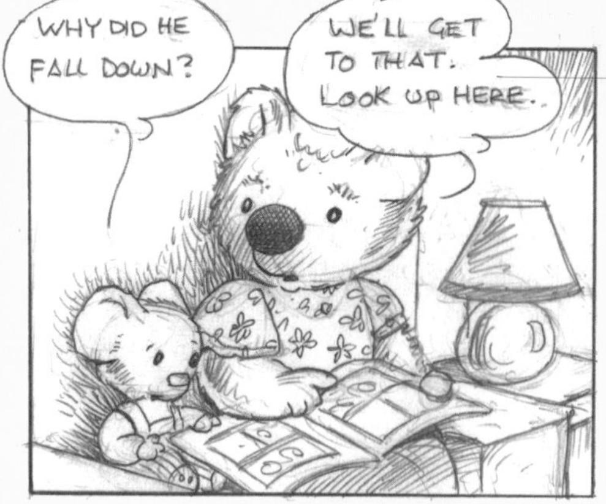

WHY DID HE FALL DOWN?
WE'LL GET TO THAT. LOOK UP HERE.

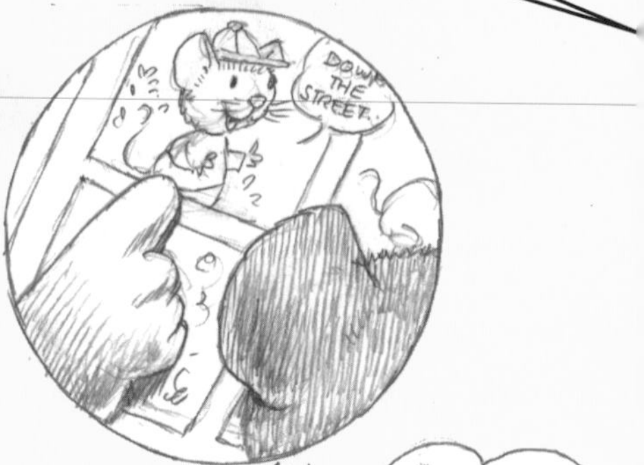

DOWN THE STREET.

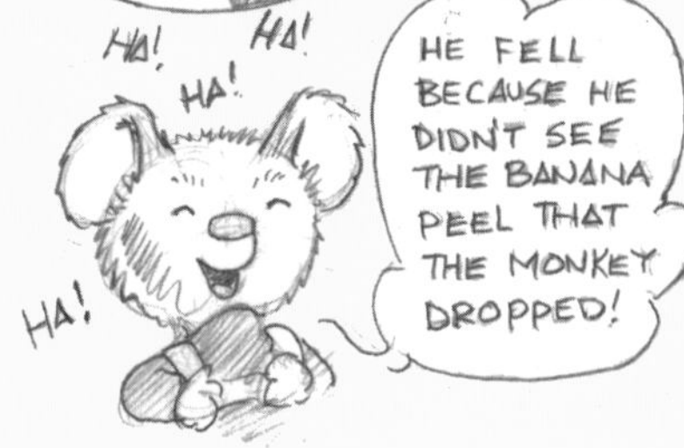

HA! HA! HA! HA!
HE FELL BECAUSE HE DIDN'T SEE THE BANANA PEEL THAT THE MONKEY DROPPED!

4 LET THE PICTURES TELL THE STORY

In a comic, you can often read the story even if you don't know all the words. Encourage young readers to tell you what's happening based on the facial expressions and body language.

5 GET OUT THE CRAYONS

Kids see the hand of the author in a comic, and it makes them want to tell their own stories. Encourage them to talk, write and draw!

Get kids talking, and you'll be surprised at how perceptive they are about pictures.

6 LET THEM GUESS

Comics provide a large amount of context for the words, so let young readers make informed guesses, and don't overcorrect. In this panel, the artist shows a pirate ship, two pirate hats, and two pirate flags the first time the word "PIRATE" is introduced.

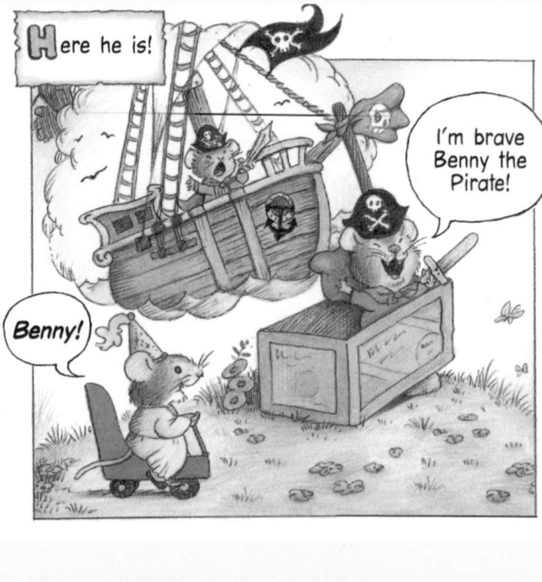

Here he is!
I'm brave Benny the Pirate!
Benny!